"It would be worth i...

Zoey's eyes widened. "What makes you so sure?"

"The chemistry between us." Cam gestured back and forth. "You've felt it. I know you have."

"Prove it," she said.

"What?"

"Prove we've got chemistry worth pursuing. Give it your best sh—"

Cam pulled her to him, lowered his head and locked his lips to hers. Yeah, he kissed her. Right there, right then, in the perishable cargo area of one of the largest airports in the world. Reliable, hardworking, you-need-to-loosen-up Cameron MacNeil kissed a woman he'd known less than an hour. Deeply kissed. Passionately kissed.

Warmth raced through him, with desire close behind.

Zoey gasped, drawing his breath from him.

Wow, did they have chemistry. Combustible, take-cover chemistry.

She tasted good. She was warm toasted malt and wheat. He also detected a little added unidentifiable spice, a secret Zoey spice that kept it interesting. If he could bottle her, he'd have a winner.

Cam lost himself in the slow, thorough kiss. Gus was right again. Cam needed a woman—but not just any woman.

This woman.

Dear Reader,

Have you ever been stuck in an airport? Several years ago I was stranded at SeaTac. After standing in line for hours, I learned that it would be five days before I could fly home. Fortunately, I didn't have to spend them in the airport. Others decided not to wait. I watched total strangers form groups and rent cars and vans so they could drive to another airport. I knew that someday I was going to write a book where the hero and heroine did the same thing. *Taken by Storm* is that book.

After a blizzard cancels their flight, Zoey and her sister's champion Afghan hound accept a ride with Cam, a handsome Texas brewer. Thus begins their road romance as they battle time, snow and a neurotic dog—and fall in love anyway. I hope you enjoy their adventure!

Best wishes,

Heather MacAllister

www.HeatherMacAllister.com
www.Facebook.com/HeatherMacAllisterBooks
www.Twitter.com/Heather_Mac

Taken by Storm

—

Heather MacAllister

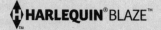

Recycling programs
for this product may
not exist in your area.

ISBN-13: 978-0-373-79810-0

TAKEN BY STORM

Printed in U.S.A.

ABOUT THE AUTHOR

Heather MacAllister lives near the Texas gulf coast, where, in spite of the ten-month growing season and plenty of humidity, she can't grow plants. She's a former music teacher who married her high school sweetheart on the fourth of July, so is it any surprise that their two sons turned out to be a couple of firecrackers? Heather has written over forty-five romances, which have been translated into twenty-six languages and published in dozens of countries. She's won the Romance Writers of America Golden Heart Award, several awards from *RT Book Reviews* and she's a three-time Romance Writers of America RITA® Award finalist, but she's most proud of the notes from readers saying her stories made them laugh. When she's not writing, Heather collects vintage costume jewelry, and loves fireworks displays and sons who answer their mother's texts. You can visit her at www.heathermacallister.com, like her at www.facebook.com/heathermacallisterbooks, or follow her at www.twitter.com/heather_mac.

Books by Heather MacAllister

HARLEQUIN BLAZE

To Sherry and Kevin Fontenot

May you have a life filled with romance and happiness

1

ZOEY ARCHER WAS three steps away from her desk when the phone rang. Three steps toward her first weekend off in months. And she hadn't even left early, unlike all but one of her colleagues—the weird girl who spoke to people in a variety of accents and dressed in monotone outfits that didn't quite match under the greenish fluorescent light of the Loring Industries customer-service call center, deep in the heart of Texas.

The phone chirped again. Weird Girl shot a look at Zoey, grabbed a pinkish red jacket and ran out the door before the call could roll over to her section. Zoey wondered what life Weird Girl was running to because nobody chose working in a megacorporation's customer-service call center as a career. This was a survival job, one people kept to pay a few bills until they became successful in their *real* lives.

Zoey's real life, however, was…complicated, meaning she'd taken a few wrong turns on the road to success. She wanted a career where she could help people, but, to be honest, many people no longer wanted her help—specifically, those she'd encountered in the health-care and teaching professions, the food-service and travel industries and anyone who ran a children's summer camp. People loved her, at least in the beginning. She was described as sincere, enthusiastic and full of great ideas. She'd also been called impulsive, but Zoey considered herself proactive. She took charge and made things happen.

Unfortunately, some of those proactive things had been mistakes. Huge mistakes. Expensive mistakes. Her intentions had been good, but the execution was flawed, as they say.

But she was always a big girl about it. When she messed up, she accepted responsibility, apologized, tried to fix whatever she'd gotten wrong and paid for any damage, even when she couldn't afford it. Did she learn from her mistakes? Sure. Did she get a chance to prove it to those she'd wronged? No.

She understood why people were reluctant to give her a second chance. Money couldn't fix everything and some opportunities were lost forever.

However, recommending a competitor's product because Loring's cream caused a rash had not been a mistake…even though going off script had landed her on the night and weekend shift in the shipping center to prevent her from talking to actual customers. And it had cost her a boyfriend, who hadn't liked the fact that she worked every night. But even that hadn't been a mistake.

Management had meant the suspension as a punishment, but Zoey had become inspired while filling thousands of orders during the Christmas season. She happened to know a thing or two about skin care. For years, she'd mixed her own organic moisturizers and soaps. The complaints she'd fielded in the customer-service call center had shown her that the world needed her products. *That's* how she could help people—by offering them a better alternative. Nobody would get a rash from her creams and lotions, unlike the cheap chemical cocktail Loring put out.

Not that the Loring Quality Control Department had appreciated her input. Well, they'd had their chance. They'd pay attention to her when she started selling her Skin Garden products online, and word of mouth created a huge demand. In fact, she was going to go home right now and mix up a new batch of lemon–olive oil balm.

Never mind that it was Friday night, party night. Zoey didn't have anyone special to party with, anyway. And honestly? She wasn't all that torn up about it. She hadn't had a date since Justin—wait, Jared…or was it Josh? Whoever it had been didn't matter. All her ex-boyfriends had been fixer-uppers who she'd tried to fix—er, help. Ultimately, they hadn't wanted her help, either.

So no more wasting her life on time-consuming, energy-zapping relationships. No more distracting boyfriends. From now on, it was going to be all about Zoey.

The whole weekend stretched ahead of her. Zoey hung up her headpiece, slung her purse over her shoulder and headed for the door. Now that it was January, Loring no longer offered twenty-four-hour live customer service, as though people magically stopped having problems on nights and weekends. Zoey vowed that Skin Garden would offer full-time customer service, even if she had to answer the phone herself.

Speaking of… The phone warbled again and guilted Zoey into stopping. A person who called after hours—and seven minutes after five counted as after hours—would have to wait until Monday morning to talk to an actual customer-service agent about whatever issue they were having with whichever one of the thousands of products Loring Industries manufactured for their dozens of brands.

Someone probably had a rash.

Zoey could see the blinking light at her station out of the corner of her eye. It wasn't as though she was abandoning someone in their hour of need. The customer could talk to a company rep through a live chat on their computer. Unless she was a "legacy customer," Loring's term for those who didn't use computers. Zoey swallowed. What if the caller was some poor, elderly widow with a bad rash who could barely read the contact number on the label because her eyes were swelling shut? She wouldn't have a computer, and even if she did, she certainly wouldn't know how to do a live chat. Besides, the *live* part was likely another computer, anyway, at least for the first few levels....

Damn her work ethic, anyway. Zoey hurried back to her station and snatched up her earpiece.

"Loring Industries. How may I help you today?" Technically, the extent of Zoey's help was routing the call to someone else who could do the actual helping, registering complaints or sending out coupons. Lots and lots of coupons. She was very generous with coupons. She was the coupon fairy.

"Zoey Archer, please."

It was so unusual to hear herself asked for by name that it took Zoey a few beats to recognize her sister's voice. "Kate? Is that you?" No wonder the call hadn't rolled over. Her sister had dialed Zoey's extension.

"Oh, Zoey. Thank goodness!" Kate exhaled in relief. "I tried calling your cell, but you didn't answer."

That's because Zoey kept her phone on vibrate and hadn't checked it yet today. Call-center operators weren't allowed to make personal calls while at their station. Only during breaks. Or emergencies. Kate knew that.

Which meant... A sick feeling settled in Zoey's stomach. "What's wrong?"

"Nothing's *wrong*..."

Alarmed, Zoey had been smashing the earpiece into her head. Taking a calming breath she adjusted the rest of the headset as Kate continued, "It's just…"

Clearly Zoey was going to have to coax it out of her. "Just what?"

"Alexandra of Thebes has gone into heat."

These were not words Zoey had expected to hear at her customer-service call station at Loring Industries. And Zoey had heard *lots* of strange words in the Loring Industries customer-service call center. "Uh…okay."

"Ryan and I are in Costa Rica! Remember, Zoey?"

"Right—the wedding is this weekend." Friends of Kate's were having a fancy destination extravaganza. Kate and her husband, Ryan, had introduced the couple and both were in the wedding party. "Are you having a good time?"

"Zoey." Her sister sighed and there was a whooshing sound as she partially covered the mouthpiece. "I told you this was a bad idea," she said to someone in the background.

"I heard that." Zoey steeled herself against the automatic guilt that flooded her every time she heard her name spoken in that tone of resigned disappointment accompanied by a faint sigh the speaker didn't bother to hide.

Some people were late bloomers, and others bloomed early and withered fast, she reminded herself. Except Kate. Kate had bloomed early and perfectly and showed no signs of withering. "Kate, so far all you've told me is that one of your dogs is in heat and you two are in Costa Rica. I haven't heard an idea yet."

"Zoey! You know Alexandra's not our dog."

Actually, she didn't. "You have a bunch of dogs. I don't remember all their names." Her sister and brother-in-law owned a kennel and bred dogs. Big, hairy ones.

"We're talking about *Alexandra of Thebes*."

"I—"

"*The* Alexandra of Thebes."

It was clear that she should be impressed by the name, but show dogs weren't Zoey's thing—that would be her sister and Ryan's thing. "I don't really keep up with the dog world," she said carefully. Not since she'd temporarily lived with Kate and Ryan and had tried helping at the kennel. It hadn't gone well.

"Obviously not, or you would know she's not only won every breed title for the past two years, she's also been named Best in Show at every national competition worth winning—"

"Okay! I get it. Is she one of those big hairy white dogs like Casper?" Kate and Ryan had been talking about Casper for the past year and a half. Their lives revolved around the dog. Zoey couldn't avoid hearing about Casper and his shows and his ribbons and his trophies and his diet and his hair-grooming routines even if she tried. And she had tried. Oh, how she'd tried. Kate spent more time grooming that neurotic dog than she did herself.

"An Afghan hound, yes," her sister confirmed. "But not all Afghans are white."

Kate wouldn't have called her at work unless she needed something. And she wouldn't have called Zoey unless she was desperate.

"Alexandra's puppies will be very valuable, even more valuable if the sire is also a Grand Champion. It's been our dream to get one of her puppies, but we never imagined Martha—she's Alexandra's owner—would invite Casper to breed with her!"

Misplaced pronouns gave Zoey a highly inappropriate visual. "Uh…congratulations."

"It's an unbelievable honor. Especially since Casper isn't a Grand Champion. At least not yet. He needs a lot more points." Kate sounded as though she was hyperventilating. "The Moorefield show isn't until the week after next. Martha must think Casper's chances are really good—at least Best in Breed, if not Best in Show! Alexandra has always been his main competition, but Martha pulled her out of the show because she thought she'd be in heat then and she wants to breed her. Only it seems she's early."

"It's happened to all of us at one time or another," Zoey murmured.

Her comment went right over Kate's head. "Oh, my gosh, we've never had a Best in Show!"

In the background, Zoey heard Ryan telling Kate to calm down. Her older sister had always been tightly wound.

While Kate breathlessly babbled on about possible fame and fortune, the massive LED clock over the doorway helpfully flashed the passing seconds. The overhead fans slowed and automatic timers clicked half the lights off in preparation for the weekend. Zoey was alone in a huge room with empty cubicles and no windows. She couldn't even see if it was raining or not. But she did know Kate wanted a favor and that she was stalling.

"I can't believe this is all happening *now*!" her sister gasped.

Zoey could. Crazy stuff always happened to her, why not Kate for once? "Kate, do you need me to take Casper to his booty call? Is that what this is about? Because I'll do it. You know I will."

Kate inhaled. "I…"

The silence stretched and Zoey understood why. Unfortunately, her reputation as the family screwup was well deserved. She always had great intentions and great plans, if she did say so herself. It's just that the execution rarely went according to Zoey's plans, and after things fell apart, she'd had to call on the safety net of her family and friends—and credit-card companies—more than once.

She owed Kate and Ryan big time for letting her live with them for a few months when she'd run out of money a couple of years ago. She'd promised them that she'd earn her keep by helping as they established Ryka Kennels.

A memory flashed of a hot day, a fresh asphalt drive and tar embedded in dog hair. Never again would Zoey make the mistake of underestimating the wily intelligence of the Afghan hound. Could it be that Kate was about to give her a chance to prove it?

"It's asking a lot," Kate hedged, and Zoey knew she was trying to think of any other person she could ask. All of her friends were probably at the wedding in Costa Rica, too. "You'd have to fly to Virginia to get Casper and then take him to Merriweather Kennels, which is outside of Seattle."

"I'll do it. Gladly. Just tell me where and when."

"I appreciate that, but you might have to take off as much as a week of work."

"That's okay. I can get someone to cover for me." Zoey would have to pay someone on Loring's temp list, but it would be worth it to rescue her sister for once.

"You know, maybe it would be better if Ryan came back…What? Ryan! All right, fine! *I'll* go home and *you* can tell Lindsey why she's short a bridesmaid!"

The next voice Zoey heard was her brother-in-law's as he took the phone. "Hey, Zoey, thanks for helping us out. I really appreciate it. I'll book the tickets, but I have no idea what kind of flights I'll be able to get. I'll try to get one out of Austin, but you may have to drive to Houston."

"It doesn't matter." She meant it. For once, Kate-the-perfect needed *Zoey's* help. "However it works out."

"Thanks. Uh…Kate is going to talk to Phyllis—she's the woman who's running the kennel while we're gone—

and she'll have all the instructions ready when you get there."

"And promise me you'll follow them *exactly!*" Kate yelled from the background. "Even if you think they're stupid. Even if you think you know a better way. In fact, don't think at all. We'll do all the thinking."

Her sister didn't trust Zoey's judgment. "Tell Kate to relax. I can do this." She had to.

The truth was that Kate wasn't the only one who doubted Zoey. Lately, Zoey had been doubting herself. She tried not to, tried to shake off her mistakes, tried to look at them as learning experiences, but her inner pep talks weren't working anymore.

She had to do this for herself, not just for Kate. Zoey had to succeed at *something*. Once she tasted success, she could start her skin care business with confidence.

"It'll be a pain," Ryan warned. "Since it's close to the date of the next show, you'll have to maintain Casper's daily routine. It's all about the coat. You might even have to—"

"Don't talk her out of it!" Kate's voice was panicked.

"She has to understand what she's getting into." Ryan's voice was filled with calm reasonableness.

Guess which made Zoey nervous? "Hey!" she said to get their attention. "I'm on my way home. Why don't you call me in a couple of hours after you've worked out all this…stuff."

They were still arguing as the call disconnected.

Although she knew she shouldn't, as she walked to the parking garage, Zoey compared her life to her sister's. Yeah, Kate was only two years older, but she had a husband and a house and a car that was less than ten years old and had a heater that worked. Although having a working heater in this part of Texas wasn't that big of a deal.

Kate also owned a successful business that was about to hit the big time.

Her sister deserved the success. Really. She and Ryan worked hard.

I work hard, too, Zoey thought. Except everything Kate touched turned to gold and everything Zoey touched turned to poo. It had always been that way. Her parents had expected another Kate—and got Zoey. In school, teachers expected another Kate—and got Zoey. So Zoey learned to avoid following in Kate's footsteps while she tried to find her own success.

So far, all she'd found was failure.

But not this time. Zoey gripped the steering wheel on her fourteen-year-old Honda Civic. Here was the perfect opportunity to figure out where she'd been going wrong. Kate and Ryan were making all the plans, all the arrangements. Kate would leave incredibly detailed, nitpicky instructions telling Zoey exactly what to do and how to do it. She'd have a blueprint for success. All Zoey had to do was follow it.

Success breeds success. Zoey grinned as she backed out of her parking space. Or in this case, Afghan puppies.

CAMERON MACNEIL CAREFULLY packed a bottle of MacNeil's Highland Oatmeal Stout in bubble wrap. Standing next to him—and not helping—was his annoyed cousin Angus.

"I don't see why you want to bring in an investor," Angus said. "And judging by your caginess, he's no Mac-Neil."

"Do you know a MacNeil with the kind of money we need who we haven't already hit up?"

Instead of answering, because the answer was "no," Angus chugged the rest of the bottle of stout he'd nabbed. Highland Stout was not a chugging type of beer, but the nuances of hops and yeast escaped Angus. The alcohol content did not.

"Easy," Cam warned. "We don't have a lot of that batch left."

"Make more." Gus reached for another bottle, but Cam grabbed his wrist and guided it to the Highland Spring Bock they were about to release.

"The stout is a seasonal. Try this one."

"Dishwater," Gus grumbled and went for the high alcohol Pumpkin Porter they'd experimented with last fall. Cam let him have it. He didn't like the way the porter tasted, although a lot of folks did. There seemed to be some unwritten rule now that all brewers had to come out with a pumpkin beer in the fall. Personally, Cam didn't think the mixture did the beer or the pumpkins any favors. And don't get him started on raspberries. Their Highland Heather Honey beer had promise, but so far, he wasn't satisfied with the recipes they'd developed. But he would find the right one eventually. At least the failures weren't wasted, he thought with a glance at Angus.

"*That's* what I'm talking about," Gus said after a deep swallow. "Och, laddie, ye just gotta have faith in y'self."

Cam shook his head at the accent. Cam's problem wasn't a lack of faith; it was a lack of help at the brewery. He considered a moment and then packed a bottle of the Pumpkin Porter to take to Seattle.

"What?" Gus tilted the bottle to his mouth.

"The accent. It wasn't that strong when you lived in Scotland."

"Lassies luuuuuv m' accent. It's part of the package." He burped.

"Is that part of the package?"

Gus waved it off. "It shows I'm a man who enjoys life."

"Or at least beer."

Gus turned the bottle until the label faced Cam. "Yeah, and whose mug is that on the label, I want to know?"

A swath of the MacNeil tartan ran across a corner of the label behind a smiling, red-bearded man with a receding hairline—Gus. Although in current versions of the label, his hairline had been considerably filled in, thanks to the miracle of digital photo enhancement. "We don't want the lads to be associating drinking beer with losing their hair," Gus had explained virtuously.

Cam nodded to the label. "Are women really and truly impressed by that?"

"A man capable of fully appreciating a good brew is a man capable of fully appreciating a good woman."

"And that line actually works for you?" Cam decided to add another bottle of the Pumpkin Porter to the wooden sample crate. Gus actually did know his beers. He was the front man for MacNeil's Highland Beer. Cam was the everything-else man.

Gus patted his belly. "You'll never get a hit if you don't swing your bat, if ye get what I'm sayin'."

Cam gave an unwilling laugh. "I do, but I wish I didn't."

"Yer just jealous because the ad folks didn't pick yer pretty face for the label."

"I don't want to be on a beer label."

"Och, surprised ya, though, di'n't it? That they picked me over you."

"Not really."

"Oh, come on, Cam. Give a guy a break," Gus said, dropping the accent. All but the part that was real, anyway. "When I'm hanging around you, I need some kind of an edge. Women won't notice me otherwise." He took another sip of beer.

Cam glanced down to where Gus's huge belly draped over his kilt. His cousin must have put on thirty pounds since they started brewing beer commercially a couple of years ago. Aesthetics aside, it was also a health issue. And Gus believing his beard disguised his double chin wasn't good, either.

"What are you staring at?" Gus spread his arms wide. "The kilt?"

Actually the stomach, but now wasn't the moment to get into it. "That's not a kilt."

Gus looked down. "What would you call it then?"

Cam hid a smile. "A denim skirt."

"Get with the times, Cam. Not all kilts are plaid wool anymore." Gus drained the rest of his beer. "And I gotta tell you, they're a helluva lot cooler for a Texas summer."

He wiped his shining forehead on his sleeve. He was sweating in the unheated brewing room in a Texas January. It didn't bode well for when it actually was summer in Texas.

"The ladies do like a man in a kilt," Gus informed him. "Now, I know what's running around in that head of yours."

Probably not, Cam thought.

"But here's the way I see it—on our next Saturday tour, you put on a kilt and flash those dimples of yours—"

Cam hated his dimples.

"—and maybe a little more—" Gus twitched the hem of his kilt and laughed uproariously, holding his belly. He looked like a Scottish Santa Claus. "And every female in the room will buzz right on over to you."

"Cut it out, Gus."

"It's true!"

"Then why would you want me to wear a kilt?"

"To get it over with. You take your pick of the girls and free up the others for the rest of us mortals. The women will be disappointed, but then they'll see me in a kilt and if they squint real hard, and sample enough of the beer, they'll be reminded of you."

"I must be getting tired because that makes a weird kind of sense." Cam arranged curly wood shavings around the bottles for padding. He'd remove the bubble wrap and fluff everything up for a nice presentation after he got to Seattle.

"And it solves another problem."

Cam reached for the crate's top. "That would be?"

"You don't have a woman in your life."

"Gus…" They'd been over this, although why Gus felt Cam's love life, or the lack of it, was his business escaped Cam.

"I know. You don't *want* a girlfriend. You don't have *time* for a 'relationship.'" Gus used air quotes, which Cam ignored. "But you being unattached gives all the lassies hope. And if they have hope in their hearts for you, they aren't going to fully appreciate my magnificence."

"I apologize for the fact that my lack of a girlfriend is impacting your love life." Cam fit the top onto the presentation crate and admired the MacNeil logo burned into the corner. Without Gus's face. That had been one argument Cam had actually won.

Gus set the empty bottle on the table next to Cam's box of samples. "It affects more than that. And more than me. We're *all* well aware you don't have a woman in your life. You *need* a woman."

"I *need* to hire help at the brewery."

"Why hire someone when you have your family? I'm not talking about a *relationship*." Gus moved his arms in a big circle. "Just a short acquaintance. A night or two, even." Cam picked up a rubber mallet and Gus backed off, palms outstretched. "That's all I'm saying."

It probably wasn't, knowing Gus.

"A woman might even be able to change your outlook.

You might see things a little different and not want to expand the brewery and take on all that extra work. You're already complaining about the work you've got."

"Expanding shouldn't cause much extra work. Not with all my brothers and cousins around to help." Cam was being sarcastic, but he didn't expect Gus to notice.

"Cam." Gus touched his arm. "Leave things be."

"I can't." He faced his cousin. "MacNeil's is too big to be a family hobby, but we're not big enough to get any kind of regular distribution. We grow, or we fold."

"You have to relax, Cam. Enjoy life."

If he did, there wouldn't be a MacNeil's, a point he hoped to make while he was gone next week. "You mean I should stand around and drink beer and spout clichés in a fake accent while wearing a skirt, like you?" Cam immediately regretted his words—not because they weren't true, but that he'd indulged himself by saying them.

Gus didn't take offense. "And didn't that nonsense you blathered just prove me point about you needing a woman?"

Let it go, let it go. But he couldn't. "It was a little harsh, but it wasn't nonsense."

"Och, laddie." Gus shook his head.

"Fake accent."

"It's the excess man juices bubblin' around in yer blood talkin'."

"You did not just say 'man juices.'" Cam whacked at the metal fastening staples. They sank into the wood and started a tiny split. Great.

"It's the truth. Your juices are all backed up with no place to go, so they've spilled over into yer blood, where they've been bubblin' and fermentin'." Gus illustrated this by wiggling his fingers.

Cam whacked another staple into the box.

"Until one day, you'll see a female and you'll blow your top, just like that batch of summer ale the first year."

"Gus." A corner of Cam's mouth twitched.

"It's why men make poor decisions with the wrong women." Gus took the mallet from him. "Or they let the right one get away 'cause they've got no finesse and scare her off." He expertly pounded in the final staples and tossed the mallet onto the table. "Or they go begging to some Sassenach for 'expansion' money so he can share in the profit after we've spent years establishing ourselves, doing all the hard work, developing and testing recipes and pouring free beer down the gullets of the public so they'll get a taste for it."

Cam clapped. "Very dramatic."

"But true."

"Agreed. But now that they've got a taste for our beer, we've got to supply it to them. Here's the thing. The Beer Barn in Wimberly is getting rid of their tanks. They're outsourcing the house brew."

Gus gasped. "That's sacrilege!"

"That's opportunity. For us." He gestured for Gus to hand him a foam cooler. "I want to buy the tanks and then lease the space so I can leave them there for now. We brew more of our two bestsellers there *or* we brew one of ours and make a pitch to brew the Beer Barn's house label in the other."

"Och, laddie, yer a crafty one." Gus waggled his finger, then turned shrewd. "Who's our competition?"

"It doesn't matter if we slip in with a cash offer."

"Ah." Gus gave him a long look. "But we don't have the cash."

Cam shook his head. "Not yet. But if my meeting in Seattle goes the way I hope it does, I'll have the money."

Gus shrugged. "Bringing in an outsider will have to come to a vote, and the lads won't agree."

He meant Cam's two brothers and assorted cousins for whom the brewery was more a source of fun and free beer than a business. "Then the 'lads' can take over. Because I'm tired of going without. I'm tired of being poor. I'm tired of never having a day off. I'm tired of living paycheck to paycheck."

Once Cam got started, the words just rolled out, louder and louder. "I'm tired of driving an old car. I'm tired of paying credit-card interest. And I am bloody well tired of not having a girlfriend!" His voice echoed in the cavernous space.

Gus didn't even blink. "Fair enough." He opened the door to the visitor fridge and stared inside. "You never said who your investor was."

"A guy I know from school." The crate squeaked as Cam forced it into a cooler. "A computer geek who sold an app to Apple or Google or some big company." Cam taped the lid on to make sure it stayed put. "He thinks owning part of a brewery will make him seem hip."

Not that Cam intended to sell any part of MacNeil's. He was hoping to sell naming rights for a custom-brewed beer, but if his trip made the family nervous, so much the better.

Cam set the cooler into the shipping container for the plane and added more padding. It might be overkill, but he didn't want to chance the bottles breaking or freezing.

Gus was still staring into the fridge. "I suppose I could live with an outside investor." He shut the fridge door without taking a beer. That meant he was still thinking. The thing about Gus was that he wasn't stupid, although he encouraged people to believe so. But he *was* less smart after a few beers.

"As long as you aren't asking us to get into bed with one of those infernal Campbells."

Gus needed more beer.

Cam bent down to grab a double handful of the packing shavings.

"What's this investor's name?" Gus asked.

Oh, here we go. "Richard." Cam straightened. "Hey, as long as you're standing there, would you slap a label on the box?"

Gus took his time peeling the backing off the label. "Would ye be referrin' to the aptly named Dick Campbell?"

"He prefers Richard."

"I'll bet he does."

"Campbell is a common last name."

"Common, yes."

"Gus! Don't go there. Clan rivalries are fun at the Highland Games, but nobody takes it seriously."

"I take it seriously." He did.

"Then be serious in Scotland." Cam held his gaze. "This is Texas. The brewery's at stake. Are you really going to fight me on this because of some quarrel our ancestors had with the Campbells hundreds of years ago?"

"If I don't fight with you now, you'll be fighting with him later." Gus slapped the label on the box. "No Campbell is going to write you a check and just stand back and let you do whatever you want with his money."

"Richard has his own business to run, and he's in Seattle. He's not going to bother us." As Cam added samples of yeast and hops to the shipping container, he was aware of Gus's stare. "Look." He turned to his cousin. "We'll invite him down and let him help us brew a batch of beer. Then we'll send him a few cases and he can give it to all of his friends. Trust me—this is only about Richard wanting to be cool."

"Trust *me,*" Gus warned. "It's about a hell of a lot more than wanting to be cool."

Cam finished taping up the shipping box and Gus reached around him to flip off the light. "Hey, what are you doing?"

"Going home. Aren't you?"

"I wish." Cam had another few hours of work ahead of him. "I've still got to check in with the volunteers for tomorrow's tour and start setting up."

"No, you don't." Gus flipped off the rest of the lights. "You're just making extra work for yourself. They know they're supposed to be here to set up."

Cam turned the lights back on. "Some forget."

Gus waved away his words. "So what if they do? Plenty of people will be around to pitch in if you need extra help. Relaaax, laddie boy. It'll all work out."

Relax. It'll all work out was Gus's standard response to Cam's concerns about the brewery. "I'll relax next week when you're the one making it all work out."

"You do that," Gus said. "And find a woman while you're at it."

2

As SOON AS Zoey got home, she flipped on The Weather Channel and started packing. Central Texas generally had mild winters, but she was flying first to Virginia, then renting a car to drive to her sister's kennel, then flying to Seattle and renting another car to drive to Merriweather Kennels. Apparently dog breeders favored rural locations.

She caught the tail end of the report: "...stalled over the Rockies. This area of high pressure is feeding all that moist Gulf air, and when it eventually moves along this line, the Midwest will be in for heavy snow, probably within the next couple of days..."

Snow. Zoey did not do snow. She didn't see snow all that often and had driven in it only twice.

While she waited for Kate and Ryan to call with her itinerary, Zoey transferred samples of Skin Garden creams into airline-approved containers. Flying all over the country was a great opportunity to test which formulas best combated dry airplane air. She even added extras to make a nice gift bag for Alexandra's owner. Word of mouth had to start someplace.

Near midnight, her sister called. "Hey, Zoey, sorry about the slop in the flight schedules, but not all the commuter planes have pressurized, temperature-controlled cargo holds. And the layover must be long enough to let Casper potty when you change planes in Chicago."

Chicago. Chicago was in the Midwest. "Hey—have you been watching the weather? There's a big storm—"

"It's January. There's always a big storm," Kate snapped.

Zoey had kept the TV on for company, and the projections had changed over the past few hours. The storm was growing and moving faster than originally predicted. Meteorologists were thrilled and trying not to show it, which was never a good sign. "Maybe you should have the woman at your kennel put Casper on the plane in Richmond and I'll just fly to Chicago and meet him there. It would save a day."

"In other words, leave the kennels unattended for hours, and then let a future Grand Champion travel by *himself?*"

"Unless there's something you're not telling me, he'll be by himself in the cargo hold anyway. You should turn on the TV. I think this storm—"

"Zoey! You promised not to think!" Kate sucked in a deep breath. *"Just follow the plan."*

Right. Zoey's plans led to failure. Kate's led to success. "I was just wondering about the effects of the snow."

"I appreciate your concern, Zoey." Ryan's voice. "But Casper needs to become familiar with you and you'll have to learn his routine. Believe me, it'll make traveling with him a lot easier."

At Chicago's O'Hare Airport, Cam watched with a crowd of cranky passengers as flights on the departure monitors changed from "delayed" to "canceled."

He should have called off his trip after waiting for hours at the Houston airport because he knew incoming flights from Denver had been delayed. Snow and ice. Hadn't Colorado figured out how to deal with snow yet? And now the storm was bearing down on Chicago. If he couldn't get a flight out, who knew how long he'd be stuck here?

Cam made his way to baggage claim to find out where the checked luggage was being stored. If it was in some unheated warehouse, then he'd have to retrieve the beer. The foam cooler would probably keep the bottles from freezing, but the samples of wort, hops and yeast weren't protected.

He stepped off the escalator at baggage claim into a solid wall of people and lines that were so long, he couldn't see the end of them. The babble and smell of overheated travelers made it hard to concentrate.

To heck with this. He'd find the climate-controlled shipments himself. Better to ask the guys actually handling the cargo than to rely on the agents at the counter, who could only repeat what they'd been told.

There weren't as many people at the end of the building where the administrative offices were located, and Cam took a moment to appreciate the lack of crowd noise. And fresher air. As some of his stress eased, he heard a dog bark. Right. Pets would be traveling in the same cargo hold as his beer. Following the signs, Cam found the area where the animals were being held. Great. Another long line.

Several frazzled owners were trying to soothe their unhappy pets, but Cam's eyes were immediately drawn to a woman struggling with a large dog wearing what looked like a shower cap and a blue jumpsuit with "Ryka's Casper" embroidered on the side.

The dog's butt was firmly planted on the floor; it did *not* want to go back into its crate. The woman gestured, clearly trying to reason with the animal. She finally grabbed the harness and slid the sitting dog toward the crate. The poor thing had probably been confined in there for hours already.

Cam and the rest of the waiting travelers silently watched as the woman struggled to remove little blue booties from the dog's paws.

"Casper, please!" She slipped off her backpack and set it next to the crate. "They're all wet. I don't even know why I bothered."

She bent over and the end of her knit scarf caught on the travel crate. As she tried to free the scarf, the dog pulled on its leash.

"Here, let me help you." Cam quickly moved forward and knelt by the crate.

The scarf was striped red and white, like a candy cane, and made him smile as he unhooked it from the wire door.

"Thanks," he heard as he straightened and came face to face with flushed cheeks, huge pale green eyes and a grateful but weary smile.

The air left his lungs as though he'd been punched in the chest. He stared, well aware he was staring, but he couldn't stop. Worse, he didn't want to stop. He'd happily devote whatever hours before his flight was rescheduled to staring at her and her sea-glass-colored eyes, her flushed cheeks and her...nose. Okay, there was nothing remarkable about her nose. He couldn't call it cute or even little. She wasn't crinkling it adorably or anything. It was just a nose. But it really looked good on her.

She did have nice skin—he noticed that. And brown hair, judging from the pieces of her bangs that stuck out from the candy-cane hood she wore. The hood appeared to be attached to her scarf, and he saw the remnants of a price sticker along the turned-up edge.

She blinked at him, and the wool fringe of her scarf moved through his fingers as she gently tugged.

"Oh." He glanced down and gave a short laugh as he released the scarf. "I guess you want that back." He stepped

away to give her space because her smile seemed a little
fixed.

The dog whined and pulled in the direction of the exit.

She didn't say anything, and Cam didn't say anything,
either, although he wanted to. He was doing well just to
remember to breathe. After months of easily chitchatting
with the public during Saturday tours at the brewery, now
Cam couldn't string a sentence together to save his soul.

"I guess Casper didn't get enough of the snow and slush,
so I'm going to walk him some more." She pointed over
her shoulder as she backed away, the dog straining at his
leash. "Thanks again."

Cam opened his mouth to offer to walk with her, but
he was afraid of coming off as stalkerish, so instead he
said, "Have fun." Yeah. That was the best he could come
up with.

He stood, unmoving, and watched the dog pull her
away. He couldn't gauge much about her body beneath
the wrinkled beige coat she wore, but her legs were en-
cased in tight jeans tucked into boots. Nice.

She stopped walking and said something to the dog.
Abruptly, the dog—Ryka's Casper, according to the ridiculous doggie coat—returned to her side and froze, head up,
tail curled and legs straight. She dug in the pocket of her
coat and pulled out red-and-white striped gloves. No. Mittens. She was putting on mittens. Cam grinned, pegging
her as one of those quirky, sexy girls. Usually, he avoided
that type because the quirkiness wore on him after a few
hours, but somehow he knew she was different. Her coat
said practical, her legs said sexy, and the mitten/scarf/hat
combo said quirky. He liked it. A lot.

Once her mittens were on, she gave a command to the
dog and they trotted toward the door in perfect step.

A show dog. No wonder he was dressed in the fancy

getup. Ryka's Casper. Did that mean the woman's name was Ryka?

Cam might have the opportunity to find out because it seemed he'd be hanging around here for a while. The customer-service line hadn't moved at all in the past fifteen minutes. He watched the overworked clerks. They had to be as tired and as frustrated as the passengers, but so far, they were doing an admirable job of hiding it. Still, if he got into line now, by the time he made it to the counter, his beer could be frozen.

He looked around for a cargo handler and noticed a black backpack sitting by the empty dog crate. Unattended luggage. Bad. Very bad, as the airport announcements warned. Over and over and over. But Ryka had abandoned it in her haste to get away from him. Yeah, he'd definitely come off as stalkerish. It would be his fault if someone stole the backpack or messed with it or reported it as unattended luggage. So Cam casually sat on the floor next to the crate. He'd keep an eye on the bag and leave when she returned.

He felt a disappointed pang at the thought of walking away from her, although he wouldn't walk far because the baggage-service line wrapped around the pet area. He could catch a glimpse of her cute nose or sexy legs, but he had to make sure she didn't catch him at it.

Cam rested his forearms on his knees, hands dangling free. A wave of tiredness smacked him and he dropped his head. He'd oh-so-carefully arranged this meeting with Richard after reading an interview in his college alumni magazine where Richard had expressed an interest in brewing craft beer. Fortunately, the Yakima Valley in Washington State was a huge hop-growing region, so Cam had mentioned he'd be in Washington visiting growers and offered to meet with Richard. When Richard had agreed,

Cam then actually had to plan a visit with a grower; Richard was just the sort of man to verify his story. Richard was also the sort of man to refuse to meet with Cam if he was late, even if it *was* because of the storm of the century.

Cam drew a deep breath and lifted his head, his gaze falling on the backpack again. A tiny edge of white paper taunted him from beneath the bag. The paper looked a whole lot like one of the temporary ID strips the airlines provided at the ticketing counter. If Gus were here, he'd move the backpack so he could read the information on it, but Cam wasn't Gus. Besides, if Ryka saw him messing with her bag, he'd have a hard time explaining his motives to her—or to whoever monitored all the security cameras trained on the area.

He'd have a hard time explaining it to himself. What did it matter who she was and where she lived?

Deliberately, Cam sought out the door where owners were being reunited with their pets and vowed to talk with one of the workers as soon as Ryka returned. It was while he watched the handler match a man's ID to a tag on his pet's crate that Cam thought to look at Casper's crate.

And there it was, visible for anyone to see: Ryka Kennels, Leeland, Virginia. *Virginia*. Not close to Texas. A kennel wasn't exactly a portable occupation, either. Neither was a brewery. And Ryka probably wasn't her name.

So much for that. Not that there had been a "that." Cam drew a deep, deep breath and exhaled in a whoosh, trying to blow away his disappointment. Just what, exactly, had he hoped would happen, anyway? After they went their separate ways, was he going to get in touch with her and say, "Hey, I'm that guy you thought was going to hit on you at the airport. You want to go out some night?" And then if she actually said okay, he'd have to fly to Virginia.

Not happening. Getting MacNeil's up and running consumed all his time and energy. The family had agreed that Cam's brothers and cousins would put up the money for the brewery and help out when they could, but Cam would run the show. So right now, the brewery had to come first in his life. When Cam started a new relationship, he was very up front about his responsibilities. Women always said they understood, but after a few weeks, when the novelty of spending Saturdays at the brewery wore off, they lost patience. Cam didn't blame them; they deserved more than he could give.

The brewery needed more than he could give, too, and convincing the family of that was one of the major reasons for this trip. If he succeeded, then maybe he *would* have time to fly to Virginia.

The minutes crawled by. The arrival and departure screens flashed a notice stating that O'Hare was closed until further notice. Not good. Televisions were tuned to The Weather Channel or news stations discussing the weather. Maps showed the middle of the country as a blob of white and blue with fringes of purple. Roads were closed. Transportation was at a standstill. He watched lots and lots of footage of stalled cars buried in snow and icy branches that had fallen on power lines.

Great. Just great. Cam got out his phone and texted Richard that his flight had been delayed due to weather. This probably wasn't news to Richard, but Cam had to give him some explanation for being late.

For the next few minutes, he checked his phone, hoping that Richard would text back right away. At some point, he became aware that the background noise had changed. He raised his head, trying to figure out what was different, and noticed people were starting to line the glass of the exit vestibule that buffered the outer doors. Beyond them, where he should have spotted taxis and shuttles picking up passengers, was a wall of white.

Just as he realized he was seeing snow, and a lot of it, and that Ryka and her dog were out in that mess, people backed away from the entrance. Ryka and the dog and a bunch of snow blew in through the automatic doors.

She stomped her feet and the dog shook himself. They continued through the next set of doors into the main area where she stopped to wipe more snow from the dog. Her funny candy-cane hood fell back and she jerked it and the scarf off impatiently and shook them. Then she used them to brush snow off her coat as Casper plopped down and tried to chew off his booties. Ryka saw what he was doing and removed them—without trouble this time. She stared at the mess in her hands and Cam smiled at the face she made before stuffing the booties into her pocket along with her mittens. She jostled her scarf once more and reached behind her neck to free her hair.

Glossy brown waves cascaded down her back as she raked her hair away from her face with her fingers and fluffed her bangs, which were hopelessly crinkled from being squashed beneath her hat.

The scene was like a commercial. It only lacked slow-motion camera effects.

She said something to the dog and tugged at the leash. Looking skyward, she shook her head, straightened and spoke a command. The dog immediately got to his feet and positioned himself at her side. Together, they jogged toward Cam and the crate in that peculiar trot used at dog shows.

Cam didn't need TV special effects. He saw them in slow motion. Ryka, her cheeks flushed and hair swinging, a dog in a goofy outfit trotting beside her…and a soundtrack. A voice from on high chanting, "If you claim her, do not leave her unattended. Keep her in your possession at all times and do not allow strangers to give her anything to carry." And to make sure he got the message, the voice chanted it in a couple of different languages.

He got the message, all right. His heart pounded and his man juices bubbled, just the way Gus said they would.

And then she noticed him sitting there and her step faltered. The wary expression on her face stabbed him in the chest; he'd blown any chance of spending more time with her.

Cam got to his feet so quickly, he became lightheaded. He forced a smile and mouthed, "You left your backpack" to her as he pointed. Understanding wiped the wariness from her face, but Cam wasn't going to push it. He raised a hand in farewell and walked blindly in the opposite direction.

"Oh, hey!" he heard but didn't turn around. He could have imagined it, and anyway, he didn't want her to think he was paying attention to her.

But he slowed. A little. Just in case.

Seconds later, he heard her say, "Excuse me," and felt her hand on his arm. He was sure it was her hand because at the touch, his skin burned beneath the leather jacket... and beneath the navy cashmere pullover his mom had given him for Christmas and beneath the shirt he wore under that. Yeah. He reacted that strongly to her touch.

Gus's words echoed in his mind, *One day, you see a female and you blow your top, just like that batch of summer ale the first year. It's why men make poor decisions with the wrong women, or they let the right one get away 'cause they've got no finesse and scare her off.*

Cam turned then and gave her a questioning look. *Finesse. Think finesse.*

"Um, thanks. Again." She smiled uncertainly. "I appreciate you watching my stuff."

"No problem," he murmured. There. Finesse. His voice hadn't cracked or anything. He was especially pleased that he hadn't grabbed her and planted his mouth on her lips, lips that were clearly made for kissing. Generous. Wide. Not too pillowy.

"I've got to ask you another favor," she burst out.

"Okay." He tried to avoid appearing overeager.

"I—" She stopped and exhaled. "Casper won't get in his crate and I've got to go to the restroom. Would you please watch him for me?"

"Sure." Cam allowed himself a smile and glanced down at the dog. *I owe you, buddy.*

"Oh, thank you!" She shoved the leash at him. "I'll be just a minute!" And she hurried toward the restrooms.

Cam watched her go, her hair rippling. She had great hair—straight, long and glossy. He wanted to run his fingers through it. He wanted to feel it against his bare skin. He wanted to lie back in bed and have it curtain their faces as she leaned down to kiss him.

He heard a frustrated sound, and at first he thought it had escaped him. But then he realized it had come from the dog, who was staring down its long nose at him, as though he could read Cam's mind.

"Hey, Casper," he said. "How's it going, buddy?"

With a tiny whine, Casper sat down.

"I hear ya." Cam looked in the direction of the restrooms. As was typical, the women's had a line and Ryka, or whatever her name was, hadn't made it around the corner yet.

"What say we walk over to your crate?" Cam said. The backpack was still lying on the floor next to it.

He started walking and the dog followed him, which

was good because he didn't want to have to drag the animal across the floor.

Once they got to the crate, Cam sat on the floor again, and the dog flopped beside him, head on his paws. Another little whine escaped.

Cam reached out to pat him. "Hey, this thing she's got you wearing is all wet."

She couldn't want her dog to stay in wet clothes. He took off the blue bonnet. "Oh, buddy. I thought the hat was bad."

Casper's fur was white, as Cam might have guessed from his name. But the hair on his head and ears was gathered in blue elastic holders. Probably to keep it out of the way. Cam scratched Casper all over his head, and if the dog had been a cat, he would have purred.

Another glance toward the women's restroom revealed that Ryka had only just made it to the corner beneath the sign.

"Okay, buddy. Let's get this off you." Slowly, Cam reached around the dog's stomach, seeking the straps. Casper obligingly rolled onto his side. Cam unhooked the clasps and peeled off the wet coat, releasing the aroma of wet dog and something sweet—doggy shampoo?

Casper panted.

The rest of his hair was also bunched with blue bands, but Cam could see there was a lot of hair and it was all white. And damp. Unfortunately, the baggage terminal floor wasn't very clean, with people tracking in the wet sludge from outside. Occasionally, the maintenance crew came by with mops, and earlier they'd placed black rubber mats by the exit, along with yellow tented caution signs.

Cam draped Casper's outfit over the crate to dry out and gently petted him, scratching between the ponytail bunches.

"Does that feel good, boy?"

Casper licked his mouth and resumed panting.

"I'll take that as a 'yes.'" Cam liked dogs, although he didn't own one. If he did, he'd never pick this breed. Too much hair.

Casper twitched and rolled over onto his back, curving himself into an S shape.

"You want a tummy rub." Cam used both hands. "This must mean you've warmed up to me. Now let's see if we can get your owner to warm up to me, too."

3

SHE HADN'T EVEN asked his name. Zoey had left Casper, Ryka's great white hope, with a man she knew nothing about. Except that he had a way of staring at her as though she was an ice cream cone and he wanted to lick her all over. She melted at the idea.

He sure was a hottie but a little intense. And she trusted him based on that? Desperate times and so on.

Zoey leaned against the cold tile walls as the restroom line inched forward. The longer the delay in Chicago, the greater the chance for failure.

Stop thinking that way. She hadn't veered from Kate's plan. This was just a pause. But if the "pause" went on for much longer, she'd have to call her sister. And she really didn't want to do that.

Finger-combing her hair at the mirrors before leaving the restroom, Zoey noticed a whole lot of dehydrated skin on the faces of the other women. Drink water, she wanted to tell them. Or maybe offer them some of her Skin Garden Rain balm. But she didn't, not with those grumpy expressions.

Speaking of water, Zoey swallowed a long drink from the fountain before heading back to the pet area. The line at the restroom had moved slower than she'd anticipated, and she felt uneasy that she'd abandoned Casper for so long. Zoey hadn't even asked the man if he had time to watch Casper before thrusting the leash at him. Obviously, he didn't have a flight to catch, but maybe he had some place to be or someone to be with. He certainly wasn't going anywhere outside the airport. She shuddered at the memory of the snow and the wind that had made her cheeks sting even though she'd slathered them with her lemon-olive moisturizing bar. It was the heaviest of her heavy-duty moisturizers, and it was travel friendly because it was a solid. It was a good thing she was testing her products on this trip because she'd discovered the bar was an awkward size and had melted into the container. That would have to be changed.

Zoey rounded the corner, eyes searching out man and dog. She found Casper, undressed, splayed bonelessly on the floor, getting a tummy rub.

Zoey had never seen the neurotic animal so relaxed. The man's hands moved over the pink belly with long, slow strokes, stopping occasionally to rub some spot with his thumbs. Very thorough. Great attention to detail. Knew to take it slow. Zoey sighed.

He also had a head of lush, dark hair in great-looking condition. It contrasted with Casper's snowy coat, especially when the man bent to murmur something to the dog. Like now.

Wow. Casper trusted him, and Casper didn't trust anybody without a dog treat or a blue ribbon.

The man didn't look up until Zoey was nearly on top of them, and then he smiled and continued petting the dog. Zoey felt a quiver in her own belly and sank to the floor beside them. "I *really* appreciate you watching Casper. I don't

even know your name." *Please don't let it begin with a* J.
"I'm Zoey." She reached over Casper and offered her hand.

"Zoey." He smiled as he said her name. "Cam."

She was irrationally relieved that his name didn't, in
fact, begin with a *J.* Then he grasped her hand and she got
a jolt of awareness. Or it could have been static electricity. They both started at the sensation, but he didn't let go.

"So that's what they mean when they say 'sparks flew
between them.'" He gazed deep into her eyes as he smiled
and held her hand. Tingles that had nothing to do with
static electricity raced up her arm.

Talk about a connection.

There was something about him that made Zoey feel as
if she could bundle up her mess of a life and toss it at him,
and he'd fix it. Not that she wanted him, or any man—or
woman, or parent, or sister—fixing her life for her. She
needed to do that all by herself. Then when she finally did
succeed at something, it would be *her* success, achieved
on her own, and everyone else would know it.

Casper raised his head and nosed their clasped hands.
There was nothing like a cold, wet dog nose to change
the mood.

"Okay, I get the message." Cam laughed lightly and
petted the dog. "He sure likes to have his belly rubbed."

"I had no idea." As long as this guy was giving them,
Zoey wouldn't mind a few belly rubs herself.

Cam looked up at her, eyebrows raised in a question.

"Casper is my sister's dog."

He nodded to the crate. "Is she Ryka?"

"No, that's the name of my sister and brother-in-law's
kennel. Ryan and Kate. Ryka. They raise and show Afghan hounds."

"So that explains the hairstyle and the outfit."

"Oh, yes." Zoey couldn't prevent a sigh from escaping. "It's supposed to keep his hair clean and from getting tangled and matted. You ought to see him when he's all dolled up for a show. Really gorgeous. Though talk about high maintenance." She examined one of Casper's paws. "Look. Even with the booties, the slush outside has stained the hair around his feet."

"That's a given with this floor." Cam stared down at the dog and gave his tummy a final pat. "I hope it was okay to take off his coat. It was wet."

"Oh, absolutely. Thank you." She made a face and dug in her pocket for the wet, dirty booties. "This outfit wasn't meant to withstand blizzards. I can't believe there isn't a designated pet relief area near this terminal. I mean, this is O'Hare." She gestured around them. "I had to take him across the street. At least there wasn't any traffic."

Cam looped his arms around his knees. "It's bad out there?"

"It's unreal. How do people live in this weather?" Zoey got up and laid the booties on top of the crate where Cam had draped the wet dog coat. Very thoughtful.

She slid a glance toward him. He still sat by Casper, apparently not in a hurry to go anywhere, and her lingering guilt about thrusting Casper on him evaporated.

"Doesn't it snow in Virginia?" he asked as Casper came over to the crate and nosed at the empty water container.

"Maybe, but I live in Texas near Austin, and snow isn't something I see a whole lot of." Zoey wasn't thrilled about giving Casper water—what went in was going to come out.

As she opened the spout on Casper's water dispenser, Cam said, "Hey, I live in San Marcos."

Zoey glanced over at him in time to catch a surprisingly wide smile bracketed by a couple of killer dimples she hadn't noticed before. Not that she was a dimple person. Or hadn't been in the past. She might be one now. A couple of beats went by, during which Casper's dish filled with more water than Zoey had intended. She closed the spigot as Casper lapped greedily. "I'm in Round Rock."

"Just a few miles up the road." Still smiling, he shook his head. "What are the chances?"

Zoey looked around at the people waiting in line and hanging out by the exit watching the snow. "Judging by all the A&M, UT and Texas Tech shirts, the chances are pretty good."

"It's the timing," he said. "The flights from Texas were some of the last allowed to land before they closed the airport."

"My connecting flight originated in Richmond. Not that it's doing me any favors now."

Zoey could feel him watching her. She wanted to be flattered, but under normal circumstances, she had to make a real effort to attract the attention of upper-tier lookers like Cam. Maybe she'd been going about it all wrong. Maybe all she needed to do to turn a man's head was appear travel-rumpled and fling a dog at him.

"Where are you headed?" he asked.

"Seattle."

"The 1:40 United Flight?"

"Yes. Well, originally." She glanced up and their gazes caught and held.

"Me, too," he said softly.

She couldn't look away, even though she knew she was sending signals she had no business sending. He sat still and unblinking, his eyes never leaving hers. They were cool blue with a hot message.

As awareness prickled through her, Zoey reminded herself to breathe. She exhaled and forced herself to move her eyes to the dog. Wow. That was intense.

She had to blink a few times before Casper came into

focus. He'd finished slurping the water and now waited expectantly. Food. He wanted food. Zoey didn't have that much with her. The rest of his special not-available-commercially blend was taking up a lot of space in her suitcase. She gave him a few bits from what she had in her bag. He looked at it and then back up at her. She gave him a little more. "That's all for now, Casper. I have no idea how long we're going to be stuck here."

"I hear that." Cam got to his feet and brushed his hands together. "Which reminds me, I should find out where they're storing the box I checked." He indicated the door where the airline workers loaded and unloaded animals and perishables. "I thought I'd try the cargo guys before standing in line."

"Good plan, and thanks for helping with Casper," Zoey told him.

"No problem." His eyes met hers. There was that intensity again, followed by a hyperawareness of him that caused a hitch in her breathing.

Impulsively, she asked, "Have we met? I mean, before?" Maybe that would explain it.

He started to say something and stopped.

"What?"

"I was going to say I would have remembered you, but that sounds like a line."

"Well, I know I would have remembered you," Zoey said. Again, impulsively. And embarrassingly. Feeling her face heat, she gestured vaguely. "Your smile. It's killer."

"Yeah?" He smiled his killer smile.

Oh, yeah.

"Still, there's something…" His eyes traced her face and Zoey willed her blush to fade. Maybe he'd think it was windburn. "Did you go to Texas State?" he asked.

She shook her head. "UT. Maybe we just saw each other in a crowd somewhere. Do you ever go to Dasko's?"

"No. I've wanted to, but I'm usually working weekends."

"Where?"

"MacNeil's Brewery."

"Right! It's outside San Marcos. I've been there."

His face lit up. "One of the Saturday tours?"

Zoey laughed. "More than one. In fact, I helped my friend Pam throw a birthday party for her husband there."

"Yeah?" His dimples deepened. Wow. When *had* dimples become sexy? "I'm the one who handles the event scheduling."

"Maybe we spoke on the phone!" The idea made her absurdly pleased.

"When was the party?" Cam asked.

"Oh, it's been a while. A couple of summers ago. I don't think the brewery had been open all that long."

"Then I definitely would have been manning the taps."

"Really?" Zoey could feel herself grinning, but then, so was he. For the first time in a long while—and for the first time in years with a guy who didn't have a *J* name— she experienced that glorious, fizzy euphoria of first attraction when you're sure the other person is experiencing the same thing.

"Do you remember the date?" Cam asked.

"No, but it was in July. It was a Harley-themed party because Pam was giving her husband a motorcycle. She wanted it to be a surprise, which meant we had to get it there. Neither of us had ever driven a motorcycle before, so we took turns driving it while the other followed in the car." Zoey laughed. "You should have seen us!"

She assumed he'd laugh with her, and he did, but the

fizz had gone flat. "Then once we finally got to the brewery, we had to find some place to hide the bike."

"And you hid it in the beer cooler." He was still smiling, but neither his teeth nor his dimples showed. She missed them.

"Yes! You remember!" Zoey said way too brightly.

"Hard to forget."

Okay, there was definitely an edge to his voice now. What on earth had she said? She'd babbled but not all that much, had she?

"It was a really hot weekend," he added, and Zoey knew he was referring to the temperature and not all the girls in their skimpy black-leather biker-chick costumes.

"Good thing there was a lot of cold beer because let me tell you, black leather in the sun is something else!"

He smiled—a polite, impersonal smile. It was such a contrast from his earlier expression that Zoey actually felt a pain in her stomach.

What had gone wrong? Had they drunk too much beer at the party? She tried to remember...no, and anyway, MacNeil's would have stopped serving them before they got to that point. She and Pam had cleaned up some afterward and had even returned with a couple of friends the next day to finish taking down the decorations and gather any trash.

Zoey couldn't figure out what had made Cam stop looking at her with that intense, hot, I-wish-we-could-do-something-about-this gaze and instead withdraw into mere politeness.

Whatever, it was gone. She should end the conversation. But did she stop talking? Did she say, "Small world" and shake her head, thank him again, and wish him luck with the baggage handlers? Oh, no. She kept talking. She kept talking because only minutes ago, this guy, this top-

tier looker, had been gazing at her with serious interest—
and it wasn't last call in a bar, so he wasn't wearing beer
goggles. But now he'd lost that interest, and she wanted a
clue as to why. A hint.

And so she kept talking about the stupid motorcycle.
"Speaking of cold, when we rolled the motorcycle out of
the cooler, the heat made the bike's metal fog. It was all
slick and wet and the chrome wasn't shiny, so Pam sent
me to find some rags so we could…"

A hazy memory surfaced.

"…could, uh," Zoey gestured with her hand. "Wipe the
condensation off."

The memory sharpened into a crystal-clear image of
a man—one who'd looked just like Cam—mopping up
a pool of beer. She remembered watching as a couple of
bottles popped their caps and beer fountained into the air.
The man she now recognized as Cam had thrown down the
mop in frustration before catching sight of her. They had
stared at each other from opposite ends of a long, open-
ended hall for a few seconds before Zoey had ducked into
the ladies' restroom, where she'd grabbed a handful of
paper towels.

For the first time, she made the connection between the
exploding beer and the bottles she and Pam had moved
out of the cooler the day before to make room for the bike.

"We did meet," she admitted. Might as well get it over
with. "You were cleaning up beer."

He nodded. "The bottles got too hot. The batch was
fresh."

They stared at each other just as they had then. "That
was the beer we moved out of the cooler to make room for
the bike, wasn't it?" Hiding the bike had been her idea.

"Yes."

"The red-headed guy said it was okay."

"Gus probably forgot what happens to metal walls in the afternoon sun."

It had been cool and shady when she and Pam had moved the beer outside, which was why they'd chosen the spot. It had also been morning. "I don't think he knew where we'd moved the beer." And to be honest, she'd forgotten all about it once the party had started. Zoey closed her eyes. "I'm sorry. That was a big mess."

"It's not your fault. Gus should have paid closer attention."

"Yes, it was my fault." She exhaled heavily and opened her eyes. "Did you get into trouble because of it?"

"No." He denied it firmly but not before a telling hesitation.

No one but Zoey would have noticed, and she noticed only because she'd become an expert at recognizing when people were hiding the true extent of her mistakes from her. Didn't they realize it only made her feel worse?

"But you had to pay for it, didn't you? Don't." She held up a hand when he started to speak. "I know you're not saying everything. People always do that when I mess up." She had a horrible thought. "Did Gus get fired? Please tell me nobody got fired."

"Gus can't get fired," he assured her quickly. "He's one of the owners. And so am I."

That was so not what she expected to hear. A name from the brewery's website popped into her mind. He'd said his name was Cam. "You're Cameron MacNeil!"

"Yeah." His smile flashed. "So it's all good."

It was *not* all good, or he'd still be showing her those dimples. "Not until I reimburse you for the beer you lost that day."

He was shaking his head before she finished speaking. "That was two years ago. Forget it."

"A year and a half, but that's not the point. I want to make it right. I can't give you back your beer, or the time you spent cleaning it up, but I can pay for the damage."

"I appreciate the offer, but it's not necessary." Cam looked down at her and a little of the interest he'd shown earlier returned to his expression. "Gus should have moved the bottles or shown you where to put them," he said. "We learned a lesson, nobody got hurt and it's never happened again, so forget about it. Seriously."

But she couldn't. "Why? You haven't."

CAM HAD TO ADMIT she was right. "Only because Gus tells that story a lot. He thinks it's funny." Cam's jaw tightened as he remembered Gus had claimed that he'd had no idea how the beer ended up outside the cooler. And now here was Zoey, close to two years later, offering to reimburse him the moment she'd learned of her mistake. It was refreshing when people accepted responsibility for their mistakes. It spoke to a depth of character Cam found very appealing.

He gazed at her determined face. Honestly, when he'd realized she was behind the Great Exploding Beer affair, he'd written her off as a pretty but thoughtless party girl. Cam met a lot of that type at the brewery, and they weren't worth the bother.

But glad as he was to know he'd been wrong about her, Zoey had become dangerously attractive.

The original idea had been to enjoy flirting with her while they were stuck in the airport and then they'd both walk away afterward. The danger was that he wasn't sure he'd want to walk away. He didn't want to walk away *now*.

"But you don't think it's funny. You're still mad."

Cam realized he'd been frowning. "Not at you." He

smiled. "You apologized, so we're good." He suspected they could be great, though, and he wanted to find out.

The timing? Horrible.

The logistics? Impossible.

The chances of a successful relationship? Not high. Especially when she should be looking at him with relief and gratitude.

Except she was *not* looking at him with relief and gratitude. More like anger and something else. He couldn't figure out what. Maybe it was just anger.

Why was *she* angry?

He'd expected her to say something like, "That's really nice of you. At least let me buy you coffee." Or dinner because what else was there to do while they waited?

Instead, she said, "We are not good. If we were good, I'd be seeing your dimples right now. But you're dimpleless."

He blinked. "Dimpleless?"

"Yeah. As soon as you realized I was the one who broke your beer, you turned colder than that blizzard outside." She gestured toward the doors and her hair whipped around, almost close enough to brush his arm. His skin tingled anyway.

He couldn't exactly tell her he was "dimpleless" because he'd felt a real connection with her and then was hugely disappointed when he'd thought she wasn't worthy. But now he'd decided she was more than worthy and was mentally complaining to himself about the timing. No, he couldn't say those things unless he wanted to sound like an arrogant jerk. A little arrogance never hurt anybody, but he wasn't a jerk. "I'm over it. You apologized. I accepted." He smiled until he felt his dimples. "See?"

"I see fake dimples."

Cam's smile became genuine. "Why are you mad?"

"Because you won't admit you're mad!"

"Because I'm not."

Her cheeks were flushed, but her eyes were a cool green that called him into their depths. Cam was so ready to answer that call. If she weren't glaring at him, he would.

The seconds ticked by without the heat fading from her cheeks. "How much?" she asked.

"How much what?"

Her arms stole around her middle and she hugged herself. "How much was the beer worth?"

"I have no idea," he said with exasperation. "But it doesn't matter. Breakage, bad batches, faulty bottling— it's all part of the cost of doing business."

And yet she was *still* glaring at him. "I don't believe you. You are *exactly* the type of man who would know the loss to the penny. Not only that, I'll bet you broke the damage down by actual cost and retail value."

"I wouldn't be much of a business man if I hadn't. But it's been so long, I honestly don't remember." A movement behind her caught his eyes. Casper had raised his head. The dog probably sensed the tension between them.

Zoey saw Cam glance behind her and followed his gaze. "Hey, Casper."

The dog thumped his bunched tail and laid his head down again. Zoey moved closer to Cam, close enough that he smelled the sweet, lemony scent of her skin. Like lemonade. "I want the retail value." She nodded toward his jacket pocket. "If you really can't remember, call and have somebody look it up. Right now."

Oh, for— "No."

She seemed momentarily startled before resolve settled on her features again. "I'm still going to send you money, so you may as well give me a figure."

This was about more than some exploding beer, Cam finally understood. *People always do that when I mess up,* he remembered her saying. "Why is it so important that you pay me back?"

She exhaled and looked away. "People get weird when I don't. They *say* it's okay, but the way they act around me is never the same." She met his eyes. "So I always cover the financial loss and hope for an opportunity to make up for any other wrongs."

Forget the money. Cam was more interested in the "other wrongs." "Are you saying you're accident prone?"

She shook her head. "I make mistakes."

"We all make mistakes."

"Yeah, well I make a lot of them. Big ones. And I'm getting tired of it, I can tell you."

Cam started to laugh but wisely reconsidered. "Don't you learn from your mistakes?"

"Of course. Don't hide motorcycles in beer coolers. Lesson learned."

Now Cam did laugh. "It probably seemed like a good idea at the time."

She rolled her eyes. "That's going on my tombstone." She traced imaginary words in the air. "Zoey Archer. It seemed like a good idea at the time."

He laughed again as he mentally filed away her last name. Zoey briefly smiled before saying, "So give me your contact info—or I'll just send payment to the brewery."

Cam heard a history of soured friendships and broken relationships in her voice. He was a complete stranger and she could easily avoid seeing him ever again, but she was insisting on reimbursing him anyway. He admired her for it, but he wasn't going to take her money. They needed to get past this.

She'd been waiting for his response and now gave a little shrug before turning toward the snoozing Casper. "The brewery it is."

"Wait." If she walked away now, they'd never be more than two strangers who met at an airport.

Zoey hesitated before looking up at him.

As he met her eyes, Cam tried to come up with a way to convince her to spend time with him. "Rather than paying me back with money, you could help me instead."

Her eyes narrowed. "With what?"

"I've got a box of samples that I'd rather have with me instead of trusting they won't get frozen in the warehouse." Cam was thinking on the fly. "It's heavy, we're going to be here for hours, and I don't want to drag it around with me. Not only that, the MacNeil brewery logo is printed all over the box and this is an airport full of bored, stressed people."

"I can see how that would make you a target," she said, and he wasn't clear if she was being sarcastic or not. She was not encouraging him, that's for sure.

"Since we're both going to Seattle, we should team up. We can take turns standing in lines and watching each others' stuff."

Zoey gazed at him, apparently thinking it over. "My 'stuff' includes a dog."

"Casper. I know. We're buds, aren't we, Casper?" Cam glanced toward the dog, whose head rested on his paws as he watched them. Casper swished his tail once. "See? He's all for it."

She gave a short, humorless laugh. "You're a brave man."

"Because of Casper?"

"No, because of your samples. You'd trust me with beer again?"

Was that the problem? He grinned. "It's packed in a crate inside a foam cooler inside a box. Completely Zoey-proof."

"Nothing is Zoey-proof. You hang around me, and eventually you'll pay for it." She spoke in a bleak tone of utter certainty.

"It would be worth it."

"Yeah, you say that now, but—"

"Still worth it," he said firmly.

Her eyes widened. "What makes you so sure?"

"The chemistry."

"What?"

"Between us." Cam gestured back and forth. "You've felt it. I know you have."

"Oh, please." She looked heavenward. "Does that line actually work for you?"

"It's not a line. It's the truth."

"Next you'll say you can prove it."

"I don't have to. Do I?"

Zoey froze. Asking her to admit to a mutual attraction was a gamble, but Cam needed to distract her from dwelling on past mistakes. He hoped he hadn't scared her off. Right now, it appeared she could go either way.

"You just met me," she said.

"That's my point." He gave her his most reassuring smile. "I want us to get to know each other."

She still stared at him, wide-eyed, and he really wished he could tell what she was thinking.

"I'm also serious about teaming up." He gestured toward the monitors, displaying that airline after airline was canceling flights. "This is going to get messy."

Her eyes flicked toward the monitors. She swallowed. Maybe he'd come on too strong and now he should back off. "Just consider it while I go get my box. We can talk when I—"

"No. No, no, no." Shaking her head, she backed away. Casper got to his feet and trotted over to her. "There's not going to be any teaming up. I have to concentrate on getting Casper to Merriweather Kennels to breed with Alexandra of Thebes. That's the plan and I've got to stick with the plan. I can't add anything to the plan."

"Uh, okay."

"You're looking at me as though I'm crazy." Zoey exhaled. "But when I get an idea or want to take advantage of an opportunity—that's when mistakes happen. Take the party. The goal was to get the motorcycle to the brewery, but then when we got there, I thought, wouldn't it be great if we hid it so it would be a surprise?" She flung up her hands and Casper's tags jingled as the leash moved. "And you remember what happened."

"Was getting stuck in Chicago part of your plan?" Cam asked.

"No, and that's why I have to be very careful. No distractions. So…it was nice meeting you and maybe I'll see you around." She stuck her hand out for him to shake.

Cam stared a moment before grasping it. He heard a snap as static electricity shocked them. Zoey's hand jerked.

Cam laughed. "See? How can you walk away from that?"

"Watch me." Zoey turned around and walked off, taking Casper with her.

"Zoey!" Cam eyed the empty crate she left behind and called, "I'm not a mistake. Walking away—that's the mistake."

She kept going. He couldn't believe she kept going. Couldn't accept that she'd need help eventually, unless she wanted to leave Casper unattended while she got food to eat and their flight rescheduled.

Cam watched Zoey walk away and felt a sense of loss all out of proportion to the amount of time he'd known her. He could contact her once he was back in Texas, but he wouldn't. Even if this trip succeeded and he got more help at the brewery, he still wouldn't have time for a relationship. Especially one with Zoey. Carving out the hours to spend with past girlfriends had been a chore, just one more thing on a long list of things. But he sensed it would be different with Zoey because he'd resent the brewery for taking him away from her.

She's right. Getting together *would* be a mistake. But still, Cam stood there, unable to look away as Zoey and Casper wove through the crowd. And then she stopped abruptly and a man talking on a cell phone almost plowed into her.

She stared down at the floor and stood for several seconds before wheeling Casper around and walking back.

Caught watching her, Cam expected her to change course, but Zoey strode right up to him.

"Prove it," she said.

"What?"

"Prove we've got chemistry worth pursuing. Because now you've got me wondering, and that's just as distracting as being around you, so why not find out? Maybe we don't have any real chemistry and I'll be worrying about nothing. So, I want to know. Give it your best sh—"

Cam pulled her to him, lowered his head and locked his lips to hers. Yeah, he kissed her. Right there, right then, in the perishable-cargo area of one of the largest airports in the world, reliable, hard-working, you-need-to-loosen-up Cameron MacNeil kissed a woman he'd met less than an hour ago. Deeply, passionately kissed.

Everything clicked for him in that moment. This was exactly where he was meant to be, at exactly the right time, doing exactly what he was doing, with exactly the right woman.

And then his mind caught up with all the data his body

had been sending it. He became aware of the lemonade scent, the feel of her shoulders beneath the coat and her lush mouth softly open against his. Especially her lush mouth softly open against his. Warmth raced through him with desire close behind.

Zoey gasped, drawing his breath from him. Cam was surprised he had any air left in his lungs for her to draw.

Wow, did they have chemistry. Combustible, take-cover chemistry. At least on his part; maybe not so much for Zoey, judging by her lack of response. But he hadn't given her anything to respond to, aside from the initial lip locking. He should fix that.

Cam loosened his grip on her shoulders and when Zoey still remained immobile, he eased his arms around her, under Casper's leash, and angled his head for a better fit.

The perfect fit. He settled in and gently moved his lips against hers, teasing his tongue into her mouth even as he feared she might bite it.

But she didn't bite it. She moaned a little. Or maybe he moaned. It didn't matter. What mattered was that Zoey was still in his arms. She'd even relaxed against him just a bit, which he took as wild encouragement.

She felt good in his arms, tall enough so that he didn't have to bend down too much. They were both wearing too many clothes for him to get a sense of her body, but she was neither bigger nor bonier than he'd guessed.

She tasted amazing. A little minty from a recent breath mint. He'd been popping them, too. But beneath that was all Zoey. She was warm toasted malt and wheat without the bitterness of hops or a sour, weak finish. He also detected a little added unidentifiable spice, a secret Zoey spice that kept it interesting.

If he could bottle her, he'd have a winner.

Cam lost himself in the slow, thorough kiss. He was

both relaxed and energized in a way he hadn't been for many months. With Zoey in his arms, he could temporarily set aside the burden he carried as head of the family brewery. Besides, it just plain felt good to let desire pulse unchecked through his body.

Gus was right again. Cam needed a woman—but not any woman. This woman.

A whistle pierced his consciousness and she jerked.

"Get a room!" a male voice called, recalling Cam to their surroundings once more.

He abruptly ended the kiss at the same moment Zoey wrenched her mouth away.

"Yeah, like they're going to find a room anywhere," grumbled another voice. "Everything's full. And if it isn't, you can't get there 'cause of the snow."

The murmuring of the crowd and the noises of the airport surrounded them again as Zoey stared at him, breathing quickly, her eyes huge. "Uh oh."

4

SHE'D BEEN KISSED. She'd been kissed in a way that made women turn to their partners and ask longingly, "Why don't you ever kiss *me* like that?" And enough people had certainly witnessed the kiss, as they were standing in a very crowded public area.

This hadn't been a first kiss or even second kiss. Probably not a third kiss, either. This kiss had been a no-holds-barred, possessive, passionate exploration. A you're-my-woman kiss. And if that was the kind of kissing Cameron MacNeil did on such short acquaintance, then, wow, Zoey couldn't wait for the second and third kisses and getting a room.

Zoey had wanted proof of the chemistry and now she had it.

"We can't ignore that." Cam spoke with quiet certainty. "Or we'll always regret it."

She shivered because she felt exactly the same way. She'd tried walking away, but something had pulled her back, and it hadn't been Casper. "Okay. As long as you understand that as soon as the planes start flying again, Casper gets all my attention."

He was nodding before she even finished. "I understand." He said nothing more, but he didn't have to. His eyes said it for him.

Zoey blew out her breath and then smoothed her bangs. "So now what?"

"Now we—" Cam broke off as something behind her drew his attention. "Sorry. Gotta go." And then he took off, hurdling piles of luggage and people's possessions and yelling, "Hey! Wait!"

So much for chemistry. Zoey watched as he ran toward the start of the luggage conveyer belt loop. The baggage handler had stepped onto the platform and climbed beneath the opening that led to the storage area. As Cam sprinted toward him, the man stepped inside and started rolling down the metal door.

The man either didn't hear Cam, or ignored him because Cam hopped onto the platform and grabbed the door. There was a tug of war before the door flew back up and the man shouted something and angrily gestured to the floor.

Zoey couldn't hear what they were saying, but she could guess.

Casper whined.

"It's bad, huh?" Sinking to the floor beside the dog, Zoey absently petted him. Casper huffed and didn't turn over. "So Cam's got the touch and I don't, is that it?"

Casper ignored her.

As she watched, Cam talked earnestly to the man, who shook his head the entire time. Eventually, he slumped and ducked into the opening, followed by Cam.

Zoey wasn't surprised. "He just doesn't give up, Casper."

Totally different from her J boyfriends. After an initial effort—and not much of one—those guys had settled in and were content to coast through the relationship and, as far as Zoey could tell, the rest of their lives. Zoey ended up abandoning her own goals as she tried to keep the relationships going. After a while, she realized she was the only one doing the work and when she stopped, the relationships coasted straight to a halt.

As she scratched at Casper's pink skin, she thought about all of Cam's effort with her. The Js wouldn't have bothered. She'd tried to help them improve their lives, but they hadn't wanted her help; they'd wanted her to improve it for them. And she had, at the expense of Skin Garden. Why had she believed helping them was more important than helping herself?

She glanced at the black opening where Cam had disappeared. Most of the people in the area were in line for baggage customer service. Cam hadn't stood in line. Cam had gone to the source. Cam was not content to coast or drift.

Casper whined again and licked at his front paw.

He was bored. Phyllis at the kennel had cautioned Zoey about Casper licking himself raw when he was left alone with nothing to do. His paws had been sprayed with bitter apple to discourage him, but going out into the snow and the soggy booties must have worn off the spray. And the bottle was in her suitcase because its contents were over the liquid limit for carry-on luggage. Great. Was she going to have to stand in line to take possession of her suitcase?

Zoey spent the next half hour trying to distract Casper with toys and lame attempts to put him through his showdog paces. The ones she could remember, anyway. They attracted a small audience of bored people who applauded politely the first ten times Zoey paraded Casper in a circle, but when there were no new tricks—or actually *any* tricks—the crowd drifted away.

Casper started giving her the I-need-to-go-outside look. With all the water he'd drunk, it was bound to happen sooner or later.

Zoey decided to make a reconnaissance mission to see if it was still snowing as hard as before. This time she remembered to hoist her backpack into place before trotting Casper to the sliding glass doors.

Outside, snow still fell heavily. Blown by the wind, it had begun to accumulate even beneath the covered areas.

"Casper, you're just going to have to hold it," she murmured and turned to walk him back to the crate.

It would be hours before the planes started flying again, and at that moment Zoey admitted she could use Cam's help. Just the thought of him made her heart pick up speed. Okay, so she'd be spending a few hours with him. That didn't mean she had to abandon her whole life and devote herself to his. She was smarter now. Hadn't she told him she'd learned from her mistakes?

That's when she saw Cam approaching from the cargo area. The sight of him made her ridiculously happy, and she knew she was in trouble.

He was carrying a large box and trailing plastic from his jeans pocket. After setting the box down by Casper's crate, he scanned the area—searching for them, Zoey realized. Searching for her. Another little burst of happiness fizzed through her.

Settle down. He's just some hot guy you met in an airport.

Then he spotted her and smiled, and she smiled back.

"Success, I see." She gestured to the box as Casper went right up to Cam and rolled over.

Zoey had never thought she'd have so much in common with a dog.

"In more ways than one." He pulled at the plastic. "Drawstring garbage bag. We can make a poncho for Casper. I found a place to take him where he'll be sheltered most of the way."

"That's great," Zoey said as Cam withdrew his car keys and poked holes for Casper's legs in the bag.

Then he knelt and fitted the bag to the dog. It was easy because Casper stayed on his back in hopes of a tummy rub.

Zoey stared at Cam's bent head, but instead of thinking how lucky she was, she looked for the catch. No guy was this perfect and still available. Something had to be wrong with him.

"You sure you don't have a girlfriend?"

"No girlfriend." He glanced up. "Why?"

Yeah, why, Zoey? "Because you seem like a really good guy."

"I am a really good guy." He patted Casper and urged the dog to stand. "But I'm a really bad boyfriend. No spare time."

"Oh." At least he seemed to realize that relationships required some effort, unlike her string of J boyfriends. "Maybe you haven't met anyone worth the time."

"Maybe you're right." He glanced up. "What about you?"

"I haven't met anyone worth the time, either. But I gave it to them anyway."

"Why?" Cam slipped the makeshift poncho over Casper's legs and tightened the drawstring.

A great question. "I guess I didn't want to admit I'd made a mistake."

Cam loosely knotted the ties and stood. "I promise you, even if we never see each other after today, the hours we spend together won't be a mistake."

He couldn't make a promise like that, but he had, and Zoey wanted to believe him more than she'd ever wanted to believe a man's promise before, so she nodded. Then she cleared her throat and gestured to Casper in his garbage-bag poncho. "That fits surprisingly well."

Cam held out his hand for the leash. "Wait until we test it outside."

"You don't have to—"

"It'll be easier if I take him while you stay here."

Kate wouldn't like that plan, Zoey cautioned herself as she handed over the leash. But Kate wasn't here.

Cam headed back to the baggage area and he and Casper hopped onto the platform. Cam knocked on the metal door; seconds later, it rolled up. Then he and Casper went inside.

Okay. Zoey would not think dog-thief thoughts because that was just ridiculous. It was what Kate would assume and, as everyone was very aware, Zoey was no Kate.

The thought of her sister prompted a guilty glance toward her backpack and the cell phone inside it that she hadn't turned on. Maybe Kate and Ryan were too busy cavorting in the sand and surf and drinking fruity drinks with colorful umbrellas to watch the news. Maybe they'd called Phyllis at the kennel to check if Zoey had left with Casper, and when they'd been reassured, had relaxed and had fun with the rest of the wedding party. Yeah, as if that would happen.

But what, exactly, was going to happen? Zoey glanced at the monitors. She couldn't read them from this distance, but the pattern of identical lines told her that nothing had changed. From people's conversations she'd overheard, there were no rooms in the airport hotels or any shuttles running to those nearby. It seemed she'd be sleeping on the floor next to Casper tonight. At least Cam would be with them. She studied the MacNeil's Highland Beer label on the box he'd retrieved and smiled to herself. Normally safety wasn't the reason she wanted to spend the night with a man.

Zoey lost herself in a daydream starring Cam and the usual reason for spending the night with a man, and although it was a very pleasant way to spend the time, she realized it had become a very long daydream. Long enough for her bottom to become cold from sitting on the floor. Long enough to wonder where Cam and Casper were. Long enough to pace, and long enough to start composing an explanation for Kate, along with a repayment plan, assuming she could discover how much a not-quite-grand-champion Afghan hound was worth. Should she calculate the repayment based on current worth or on championship potential?

CAM WAVED TO ZOEY from the conveyor-belt platform before he and Casper hopped to the ground. They made their way over to her, and she greeted them with a big, fake smile.

"Seriously?" He handed her the leash.

"What?" she asked, still smiling.

"You thought I'd stolen your dog." Cam stooped and unknotted the yellow ties from Casper's garbage-bag poncho.

"No—you...you were gone so long I was beginning to worry," she said from above him.

Cam shook out the garbage bag and laid it over his box. "You were in full-fledged worry."

She stopped denying it. "You were gone a really long time! You could have frozen solid out there!" She swung her arms around. "Casper could have run off! You could have slipped and hit your head. You could have fallen into a ditch. You could have become disoriented and lost. A car could have slid into you leaving you squashed and bleeding—and I wouldn't have been able to send help because I had no idea where you'd—"

"Here." He handed her a stack of paper towels. "All those scenarios and you never once believed I was stealing your dog?"

"The idea may have crossed my mind." She knelt and began drying Casper's paws. "It was one of many."

Cam laughed. "Sorry. I was talking to my new buddy in cargo."

"You must have given your new buddy quite a tip."

"He might name a son after me."

Zoey's head dropped and he could hear her laugh.

"Yeah," he continued. "I'll have to hit up an ATM. It was a good investment, though. I got my beer samples, a way out the back for Casper and some insider info."

"So spill." Zoey stood and looked around for a trash can for the paper towels.

"Leave that for now," Cam told her. "We need to talk."

"What's up?" She wadded the towels and tossed the ball next to Casper's crate.

"Tony, the cargo guy, has been through airport closures before, but he said this is the worst he's seen. They haven't even started clearing the runways or the roads because of the wind, and there's another storm coming in right behind this one. Nothing is getting through, including deliveries or staff for shift changes. Eventually, the restaurants will run out of food, vending machines will empty, the gift shops will sell out of supplies and people will get very, very irritable. And even when the airport reopens, it won't be at a hundred percent for a few days. Worse, this is a big, sloppy storm, so truckers are dealing with closed highways all over. Even if the supply companies could get here, they don't have anything to deliver."

Zoey gazed around them. "We should make our move now before others start realizing that." She glanced back at him. "It's nearly five o'clock. I haven't eaten in hours and I bet I'm not the only one. People are going to start mobbing the food vendors."

Cam was hungry, too. "Exactly. So how about one of

us watches the dog and our stuff while the other goes for-aging? But first, we should stake out a spot for the night. Are you okay with us sleeping together?" He hoped he sounded casually matter-of-fact.

She raised her eyebrows. "It depends on how you de-fine 'sleeping.'"

He grinned. "Any way you want to."

Instead of laughing because they were teasing, they stared at each other. The light, just-kidding atmosphere turned serious. She knew he wasn't expecting anything more than the two—three—of them spending the night in the same place, didn't she? Of course she did.

Awareness prickled his skin and his stupid man juices percolated toward his brain. If he didn't shut them out, he'd do something dumb.

Right. He drew a breath and gazed down the long cor-ridor leading back to the ticketing counters. Focus. He should focus. On something else. "We need to stake out some real estate. My guess is that all the seats are claimed by now. A corner would be best, but security will proba-bly make pets stay in this section." He nodded toward the corridor. "There's not much traffic coming through there, so let's grab some space against the wall."

In the end, Cam did much better than that, if he did say so himself. The corridor leading to the cargo wing housed the administrative offices. To avoid having office doors open into the main passageway and risking people running into them, the doors were positioned off short hallways with emergency exits at the opposite end. Cam scored a spot in front of two dark, empty offices in an entryway that was maybe fifteen feet long and seven or eight feet wide. It would be like having their own private cave with their own private red exit sign beaming down on them.

With privacy came possibilities. But he couldn't let the possibilities distract him.

"This is great!"

Cam looked down at Zoey as she tucked her hair behind her ear and smiled at him with those lips he remembered kissing. For him, the memory was vivid and fresh, but he wasn't sure if it was the same for her. Maybe she could use a reminder. Maybe she'd enjoy making some new memories.

Maybe he should get a grip, or she was going to remember him as an opportunistic jerk.

"I can't believe nobody's claimed this spot already." Zoey gave him a thumbs up. "Way to go."

Cam set his box down and concentrated on not being a jerk. "The offices could have been occupied earlier. If someone wants to get in, we'll move."

Zoey nodded. "Casper, sit." Casper sat and she eyed the small, doorless entry. "If we block off this part from the main hall, Casper will have room to move around and won't have to be tied up."

So much for sharing the long night with Zoey in their cozy little nook while Casper slept in his crate. But Zoey's suggestion made sense, even if Cam didn't like it.

The dog whined and tried to bite at one of the bands bunching his coat, but Zoey pulled his head away. "Casper, no."

How could he resent a dog? Especially because he wouldn't have met Zoey at all if it hadn't been for Casper.

Cam dragged the crate and box over to block the entryway, but there was still a gap. "He can jump that, can't he?"

Zoey ushered Casper into his makeshift pen and stood in the gap. "Sure. But he won't. He's too well trained."

Trained or not, he was still a dog. "We can find something to put there later," Cam said. "Right now, we have to track down food and supplies. Do you want to make the first foray, or shall I?"

"You go," Zoey said and sighed. "I should call my sister."

"Has your phone been on all this time?" Cam asked her. Zoey shook her head.

"Good because the charging stations have longer lines than the restaurants. Tell you what." Cam withdrew his phone and switched it on. "Give me your cell number. I'll text you so you'll have mine, too."

Zoey did, and as he drafted a text to her, he said, "I'm going to turn this off again, but I'll check it every half hour until I get back."

Zoey looked at him with concern. "You think you'll be gone longer than a half hour?"

"Definitely." Cam slipped his phone back into his pocket. "I could see inside the terminal when I walked Casper, and people are packed from one end of the building to the other."

Zoey nodded. "Good luck."

"I'll need it," Cam told her.

5

"So you're just hanging out with some random guy instead of trying to get your flight rescheduled?"

The call to Kate was not going well, which Zoey could have predicted even without the fourteen texts and voice mails that made her phone buzz and chirp like a mad thing when she turned it on.

"They aren't rescheduling anything yet, and Cam is not some random guy." Zoey had hoped telling her sister how helpful Cam had been would reassure her.

Not so much.

"We've actually met before. He owns MacNeil's," Zoey added, thinking it would make Cam sound more solid and responsible.

"What's MacNeil's?"

"It's a craft brewery outside Austin."

"He makes beer?" There was a huge sigh. "Oh, this just gets better and better."

Which Zoey knew meant exactly the opposite.

"You always do this, Zoey. You always pick these losers and believe you can make them into winners."

"Cam is different."

"You always say that, too."

"But he is." Zoey realized how she sounded, but Cam *was* different.

Before she could figure out how to convince Kate, her sister sighed again and asked, "Where are you now?"

Like it mattered. Zoey answered her anyway because it was easier than arguing about it. "In a hallway outside the animal cargo area. With Casper." She nudged him with her foot so he'd stop chewing on the blue elastic bands that held his coat in the little bundles.

"You're not even in line? *Zoey!*"

Had Kate become more scolding, or was Zoey just now becoming aware of it? "There's no point. It's still snowing. It'll be hours yet."

"But you should be in line now! Zoey, think! The longer you wait, the more people will be ahead of you!"

"You told me not to think," Zoey snapped, and she never snapped at Kate. She'd never felt entitled to.

Kate didn't notice her tone. "You don't need to think to know getting Casper on a flight is your first priority!"

Zoey had been slumped against the wall, but now she straightened and spoke calmly, quietly and firmly. "Actually, Casper's well-being is my first priority."

There was silence. Probably because Zoey wasn't often the voice of reason.

"We left Ryka at five-thirty this morning," she reminded her sister. "We've been stuck in Chicago for nearly eight hours now, and we're going to be here all night. I wasn't about to leave Casper in his crate. This isn't a kennel, Kate. Nobody's watching or caring for the animals except their owners. The handlers unloaded the crates in the claim area. All the flights were mixed together. By the time I got here, it was a free-for-all. I found Casper and moved him, and nobody stopped to ask me if I was his owner."

"That's…that's—"

"That's what happened. Yes, Kate, there are hordes of people here not following the rules. I expect they'll go feral soon. But you don't have to worry because Casper and I have barricaded ourselves in a hall cave while Cam is foraging for food. Thanks to him, we'll survive. Others might not be so fortunate."

"You don't have to be sarcastic."

"I'm not." Zoey had been staring blankly at the end of the hall and at that moment saw Cam turn the corner. An unexpected jolt of pleasure stole her breath. Yes, she'd gone from fizzes to jolts. He was growing on her. "You're lucky Cam is helping us because Casper is a lot better off." *She* was a lot better off. "I've got to go. I don't want to drain my phone's battery. I'll check in tomorrow morning."

She watched Cam approach. He looked good. Really good. Some might even say hot—and she would be one of them. The closer he got, the hotter he became and the more Zoey wanted to draw him into their little love nest and stay there until all the snow melted.

She must be really hungry, she told herself to counter this totally inconvenient lust attack. Here he was, being helpful, and if she wasn't careful, she'd make things awkward by drooling all over him. That was Casper's job. She glanced down at the dog, who'd raised his head and thumped his tail when he'd recognized Cam.

The memory of Cam kissing her exploded into her mind, and Zoey wished she could thump *her* tail.

"Hey, you're back quickly." Zoey was mortified to hear that her voice sounded breathy and all I've-been-thinking-about-that-great-kiss instead of casually pleased.

"There was a mom waiting to buy bottled water to mix baby formula so I gave her a couple of bottles I had on me and took her place in line," he explained.

"And people let you?"

"The baby was crying. That kid had a set of lungs on him." Cam handed her the bag of food as Zoey attempted to keep from going all mushy at the thought of Cam helping a mother and child. He'd gotten a good place in line out of it. But still.

"Breakfast stuff and sports drinks," he told her as she opened the bag. "It's all they had." He dug two bottles out of his pockets. "Lemon Lime Lightning and Cherry Eruption."

Zoey made a face. "At least it's liquid."

"If it tastes bad, we can empty the bottles and fill them at a drinking fountain." He held up the bottles. "Pick your poison."

"Cherry Eruption." She reached for it.

Casper whined, so Zoey fed him, and then they sat in the doorway so they had a view into the hall. "I'm going to have to get my luggage after we eat. That was the last of the dog food, and he isn't allowed any people food."

Cam peeled the paper off his breakfast burrito. "So what do you do when you're not acting as a matchmaker for dogs?"

Zoey had anticipated the question and wasn't looking forward to answering it. "I work in the Loring Industries customer-service call center."

"Because...?" He bit into the burrito.

"Because I need a job while I develop a line of organic skin-care products. I call it Skin Garden."

Cam nodded and gestured for her to continue, and she did, happy that Cam realized working at Loring was a survival job and not a career.

"Mixing my own creams and lotions is something I've been doing for years, actually. In college I started giving away some as gifts and people kept asking for more. That's when I first had the idea to make a business out of it, but I got ahead of myself and spent money I shouldn't have and…ended up in a lot of debt."

"That happens," Cam said. "I got a deal on fancy grain and accepted delivery before we had the right equipment. By the time I was ready for it, mold was growing in the grain." He dropped his head. "Expensive mistake."

"I ended up broke and homeless," Zoey told him. "My sister and her husband let me live with them while they started their kennel. And how did I repay them? By letting the dogs escape when my sister was having the asphalt driveway put in. Imagine a pack of Caspers with tar in their fur."

Cam grimaced as he looked over his shoulder at Casper. "Did you have to cut it out of their coats?"

Zoey shook her head. "Would have been easier but it also would have ended their show careers. We spent days—and I do mean days—getting the tar and the stains out. For years, I've wanted to make it up to my sister, which is why I'm taking Casper to Seattle now."

"So you'll be even with her after this?" Cam offered her a flat packet, which turned out to be a hash-brown potato patty.

"Only if I get him there and home again safely." She gazed down at the patty. "I really want to get this right. I realize how I sound, but I've lost so many jobs because I've messed up that I've forgotten how it feels to succeed at anything." She swallowed against the thickening in her throat. "This trip is a chance for me to remember what success feels like."

"And you're afraid I'll get in the way," Cam said.

Zoey nodded.

He smiled. "Then I'll stay out of the way."

And that was that. Zoey stuffed potato into her mouth to keep from begging him not to leave.

But he didn't. He dug around in the bag and came up with an oatmeal cookie. He offered it to her.

She shook her head and he broke off a piece, picked out the raisins and ate it.

"What?" he asked when she stared at him. "I don't like raisins."

"I thought you were going to leave."

"Why?"

"Because I clearly have issues. Most men would have run away by now."

"We all have issues. I've got issues with the brewery. Eat your burrito and I'll explain them to you."

So that's what Zoey did. After he finished telling her about how he'd started the brewery with his cousins and brothers—and Zoey'd become sidetracked when she realized there were more men as attractive as Cam running around in the world—she said, "You need more help but you don't want to ask for it. Why?"

She hadn't considered the question particularly profound, but Cam blinked at her before staring off into the middle distance. "I guess," he said slowly, "I'm afraid that I want MacNeil's to succeed more than my family does. That if I ask them for more, they'll stop helping at all and we'll have to close down."

"So you've been trying to do everything yourself."

"That's about it." He nodded.

No wonder he hadn't had time for girlfriends. She nudged his sample box with her toe. "What's that all about?"

"There was a guy, Richard, who lived in my freshman dorm, one of those nerdy, smart, antisocial types. He ended up becoming a dot-com gazillionaire. I read an article in the alumni magazine where Richard mentioned wanting to get into craft beer. So I emailed him and he remembered me, and now I'm headed to Seattle to find out if he's interested in investing." He gave her a half smile. "I'm hoping to raise enough cash to hire an office manager. I could really use one." He sounded tired just telling her about it.

The past hour had given Zoey a fair sense of the type of life Cam led—basically, he spent every waking hour at the brewery.

"What happens if Richard says no?"

"Part two of my plan is for Gus and the others to realize how much work is involved in running the place. Things can't continue the way they have been. If we expand, we can become profitable enough to hire help. If we don't…" He shook his head.

Zoey felt the urge to help trying to escape. It was what she always did—abandon Skin Garden so she could run to the aid of the latest man in her life. Not this time, though. This time, she was going to help herself. So instead of volunteering to become his unpaid office clerk, she asked, "When is your meeting?"

"Tomorrow morning."

"Uh…"

"Yeah. I've got to call Richard and reschedule." Cam made a face, obviously not looking forward to the conversation.

Zoey gathered their trash and got to her feet. "Sounds as though this is my cue to get my suitcase. I'll text you if anything is happening with the flights."

"Casper and I'll be here."

And knowing that he'd be waiting for her made Zoey ridiculously happy.

CAM WATCHED ZOEY until she was out of sight. Before blabbing about his troubles to her, he hadn't realized that he'd feared his family would tire of the brewery and vote to abandon it. If that happened, then all Cam's hard work would have been for nothing. He'd be out of a job, and any money gained from the sale of the brewery would be split into dozens of shares. To prevent that scenario, he'd taken on more and more responsibilities himself.

Casper had moved up to take Zoey's place beside him and Cam absently scratched the dog's side as he punched in Richard's number with his thumb.

Richard had not responded to his earlier texts and Cam had tried calling before, so he was surprised when Richard actually answered now.

After Cam explained the situation, there was silence and then Richard said, "Well, Cameron, if I'd been aware of this earlier, I could have sent my jet for you. But it's in use for the next couple of days."

As though Richard's jet would have been able to land when no other plane could. But that wasn't the point. The point was to rub it in Cam's face that Richard had a jet. "That would have been great," Cam said without mentioning the unanswered texts and calls.

"Yes, especially since I'm leaving for London at the end of the week and I'm not sure I can work you into my schedule before then. How soon can you get here?"

"Hard to say," Cam had to answer. "They haven't begun rescheduling flights yet."

"Charter a plane."

Richard knew Cam didn't have that kind of money. He just wanted to hear Cam admit it. "Plane charters aren't in the brewery's operating budget."

"I suppose it's a matter of what's important to you." A long silence followed, during which Cam remembered that he'd never liked Richard Campbell and he was pretty sure the feeling was mutual.

"Cameron, unless you get here tomorrow, I can't guarantee that I'll have time for you. Under the circumstances, I question whether you should make the trip."

He was an important, busy man. Cameron got the message. "I'm driving out to the Yakima Valley to visit hops growers anyway." And Cam was glad he could say that. "If you find you can juggle your schedule, let me know. If not, maybe we'll meet up some other time."

"I'll see what I can do," Richard finally said before abruptly ending the call.

Cameron suspected he'd never hear from Richard again.

He thought he'd be more disappointed, but he was beginning to realize that Gus had been right. Dealing with Richard and his look-how-successful-I-am attitude would have been difficult.

He could cancel with the growers and go home, except he needed to be gone longer than a day for Gus and the others truly to appreciate Cam's absence.

Later. He'd decide later because for now, he'd been given the gift of time and a woman he wanted to spend it with.

ZOEY WADDED HER clothes into a pillow as they tried to make themselves comfortable for the night. The longer she spent with Cam, the more she wanted to kiss him again, mainly to see if it was as amazing as she remembered. They'd had some moments during the evening, the kind where their gazes had caught and held and if either of them had leaned toward the other, they would have ended up in each other's arms. But maybe Cam was holding back because they were in a semipublic spot in an airport terminal. A major airport terminal. Where anyone could walk by. And did. Not often, but often enough to keep any kissing from getting out of control.

It had been hours since they'd retrieved their luggage.

Cam had also snagged a couple of airline cots and blankets, but then he'd given one of them to a woman who'd slipped on the ice and hurt her ankle—because that's the kind of guy he was. So they only had one cot, which Cam insisted Zoey take and when she'd refused, Casper had claimed it.

At the moment, Cam was stacking their suitcases, Casper's crate, and the box of samples in front of the opening to the corridor while Zoey was using their clothes and the skimpy airline blankets to pad the floor next to Casper and the cot. She could have put the dog between them, but she didn't. Now she was torn between hoping Cam wouldn't think anything of it and hoping that he would.

"There." She smiled at Cam, casually sat on the side farthest from the opening to the hall and retrieved her night creams from her backpack.

There was silence and when she checked, Cam was staring down at the navy blue pallet with unfocused eyes. Not a positive sign.

Scrambling for something to say or do before the situation became horribly awkward, Zoey raised her foot. "Help me take off my boots?"

"Sure." Cam joined her on the pallet.

As it happened, after wearing the boots for hours and hours, Zoey's feet were swollen and she really did need help taking her boots off. By the time Zoey's feet were free, any awkwardness had evaporated.

She and Cam lay on their backs, shoulder to shoulder, and talked about their lives. Somehow they got on to the topic of all the jobs and careers she'd attempted.

"I was in my party-planner phase when I met you at the brewery."

"How did you lose that job?" he asked.

"I parked in the sun and melted a three-hundred dollar bridal-shower cake."

"Somebody spent three-hundred dollars on a cake?"

"Yep. It looked like a shoe and a purse and a shopping bag."

"Still. And what happened at the travel agency?"

"I stranded a family in Paris."

Cam laughed. "That's not a bad place to strand someone."

"The wife really wanted to go to Venice, and when there was a cancellation on another tour, I booked it, but I forgot to tell them I'd changed their reservations."

"And the camp counseling? Did you lose kids or something?"

"Uh…"

"Zoey!"

"I didn't *lose* them. I just went too far on a hike. They were little and got tired and there were too many for me to carry…"

"Didn't you have a phone with you?"

"I used up the battery identifying plants."

Cam laughed. "I know it's not funny…"

"Not if you were one of the parents, and certainly not if you were the counselor who went off the assigned trail."

Cam tried to counter her mistakes with stories of his own, but ruining a few batches of beer wasn't the same. She appreciated that he tried, though.

In fact, the more time she spent with him, the more attractive he became. It would be so easy to turn and kiss him, but she didn't because she wanted Cam to make the first move. The original kiss didn't count—except maybe it did. Maybe he was counting it and now he was waiting for her to initiate. Or maybe he was waiting for a signal from her. But what signal?

Zoey wished she knew. This wasn't the usual meeting and mating dance. The music was playing, but she couldn't figure out the steps. Maybe Cam couldn't figure out the steps, either.

They should make up their own.

But first, Zoey had to get him onto the dance floor.

"My skin is so dry and itchy. I need to moisturize it," she announced.

She stripped down to her tank top and rolled up her jeans, then she slathered on a lemon sugar-cookie-scented cream. Tests proved men preferred baked-good scents, but it never hurt to verify with a real-world experience.

As she massaged cream into her calves and arms, she could see Cam's eyes following her movements, his chest barely rising and falling.

He seemed to be hearing the music and definitely wanted to dance.

All he needed was a little encouragement.

"Is your skin dry?"

Cam licked his lips. "A little, I guess."

"I could really use a guy's perspective on my avocado-lime cream." She got it out of her backpack, unscrewed the lid and let him smell it.

"Nice."

"May I?" She indicated his arms.

Cam had already taken off his pullover and now she watched as he slowly unbuttoned his shirt and set it aside, revealing a T-shirt and surprisingly well-muscled arms.

He reached for the cream, but she stopped him. "Let me."

He held out his arm. "Go for it."

Oh, she intended to. Zoey held a generous glob of cream against his skin until it warmed and then smoothed it upward. "Where did you get these muscles?" Seriously, they were like rocks covered by skin.

"Somebody has to haul around the sacks of hops and cases of beer."

"Wow." She ran both palms up and down his arms. "If guys knew working at a brewery would give them a body like yours, they'd pay you to let them work."

"I'll keep that in mind."

Zoey heard the amusement in his voice and looked up, faltering at the intensity in his gaze.

"I think that arm is done," Cam said. "You want to do my other one?"

"Oh. Yes." She'd used more than half the jar on one arm. Zoey felt her face heat as she slathered cream on his other arm.

She rubbed and stroked and smiled and leaned and stayed within kissing distance until his skin absorbed the cream and her fingers no longer slid smoothly.

Zoey screwed the lid on the nearly empty jar. "So, what do you think?"

"I like it," he said.

Their gazes caught again, but he still didn't kiss her. If she kissed him, he'd undoubtedly only kiss her back out of politeness, which would be pathetic.

Fine. Message received. Time to back off. Zoey packed away the creams, pulled on the layers she'd shed and rolled down her jeans.

"I suppose we should try and sleep." Unless he had something else in mind.

"Great idea," he said.

But there were much better ideas. Too bad they wouldn't explore them, Zoey thought as she turned away from him and tried to sleep.

THE BENEFIT OF a cot was that you avoided sleeping on the floor, yet here Cam was, on the floor. Not sleeping. He gingerly shifted his cold, numb hip and listened. From just above him—on a nice, comfy cot—he heard the sounds of soft, rhythmic snoring. At least Casper was comfortable.

Maybe the middle of the night would be a good time to visit a charging station. The lines should be shorter, and he'd used up half his phone's battery calling Richard.

He heard a shuffling on his other side. Warmth seeped into his shoulder and thigh as Zoey's body pressed against his. And just like that, all thoughts of Richard left his head to be replaced by thoughts of Zoey. Hot thoughts. Lustful thoughts. Caveman thoughts.

Cam had never had caveman thoughts about a woman before. His previous relationships had been "complicated"—yes, with quotes. They'd required So. Much. Work. And endless discussion. And mental tap dancing. It had been exhausting.

Caveman thoughts were simple. *Want woman, take woman to cave, claim woman as mate, protect and defend woman.* Also, *occasionally bring her a hunk of meat.*

Cam wanted Zoey. He'd taken her to his cave, was protecting and defending her from strange travelers and snoring Afghan hounds, and he had brought her a breakfast burrito.

His body kept reminding him he'd skipped the *claiming* part. Reminded him over and over as her rhythmic breathing gently moved her against him.

He liked her. He liked her a lot. She was unselfish, tried to help people and took responsibility for her mistakes, even when they weren't mistakes. That counted for a lot with Cam.

Cam knew all about packaging and marketing products. He'd seen mediocre beers become successful because of a clever name or label. He'd encountered people like that, too. But with Zoey, the product was even better than the very attractive packaging.

Cam eased his weight from one numb hip to the other, trying not to wake her, but she shifted away, and the only parts of his body that had been even remotely warm began to cool.

"Cam? Are you awake?"

Yes, he was awake. How was he supposed to sleep with Zoey's thigh and shoulder touching his? And her hair tickling his cheek? And the cold from the hard floor seeping into his bones? And her fruit salad of potions scenting the air? And the memory of her applying those potions in long, smooth strokes onto her arms and legs? And onto *his* arms when he'd agreed to give her a male point of view.

This male's point of view had nothing to do with the creams and everything to do with the woman who'd concocted them. He could still feel her hands on him, still see the unguarded expression on her face when her fingers had first encountered the muscles in his arms. Thanks to his job, he'd developed a set of guns and pecs that looked good in the MacNeil's brewery T-shirts. She'd noticed, and when she realized he'd noticed her noticing, she'd become adorably flustered.

He inhaled. He now smelled like guacamole and had a craving for nachos.

"Cam?"

"Mmm," he replied, which everyone knew was code for, "I'm conscious, but would prefer not to be, so don't talk and maybe I can fall asleep."

"Yeah, I can't sleep, either," Zoey said. She apparently didn't know the code. Also, her statement wasn't true; Cam was sure she'd been asleep at least some of the time her head had used his shoulder as a pillow.

He smiled. He'd like to try that again in an actual bed.

"I've been thinking," she continued, "and I've figured out what your problem is."

Unrequited lust. "Lack of sleep?"

"You're too good to be true." That didn't sound like a compliment.

"Wait till morning," he mumbled.

Zoey shifted onto her elbow and her voice came from above him. "In fact, you're so good, it's disgusting."

"What?" Cam shifted to face her, trying to make out her expression in the dim corridor lighting.

"It's what's causing all your problems at the brewery."

"How?"

"You're disgustingly responsible and hardworking to the point of saintliness and people don't like that," she explained. "Being around somebody who's too good makes them feel bad about themselves. So they either avoid that good person or try to sabotage him."

Gus came to mind.

"Then they feel guilty and resent the good person for making them feel that way," she continued. "That's what's happening with your family. You work so hard, you make your relatives feel guilty and they avoid coming to the brewery."

"Interesting theory, except their guilt doesn't keep them from stopping by anytime they want free beer."

"And you're such an unselfishly good person, you let them."

"Being unselfish has nothing to do with it. They're entitled. They've invested." Although most had drunk back their investment.

"You also rescue damsels in distress, mothers and babies and old ladies," Zoey pointed out.

"Well, yeah." Cam punched his jacket into a more comfortable pillow. "But it's not as if that happens all the time.

We're in an unusual situation. Most people are going to step up."

"Says the white knight. You're even kind to animals—maybe too kind," she added as Casper made little doggy dreaming movements, his nails scratching against the cot.

"Casper didn't give me a choice," Cam said. "I kept telling him he was in the wrong bed, but he's no dummy."

"Even he knows you're completely selfless, Cam." He detected disappointment and regret in her voice.

He gave a crack of laughter and rubbed his eyes. "You are way off base. Seriously."

She studied him. "Then if you're acting all goody-goody to impress me, you can stop now. It's not working."

"I'm not."

"Not acting?"

He shook his head. "Not trying to impress you, either."

"You aren't?"

A corner of his mouth tilted upward and he drawled, "Don't usually have to work to impress women."

She blinked and then collapsed onto her back. "Oh, no. That's terrible."

"I can try to impress you now."

"Too late. I've seen your halo."

He laughed. "What do you have against good people?"

"Being around them is stressful because there's always this pressure to be just like them. But every time I try, it's a disaster."

Judging from the stories she'd told him, he had to admit, disaster was the right word. "At least you try."

"I shouldn't," she said darkly. "I suck at being good."

"You're great at being good. You suck at doing favors. Totally different."

"See? That's exactly the thing a good person would say."

Cam propped himself on his elbow and gazed down at

her. She was staring up at the ceiling and her hair waved around her head. The ends lapped over the jacket he was using as a pillow. He idly took some between his fingers and ran his thumb over the silky smoothness, imagining the way it would feel against his naked chest. "I'm not as saintly as you think."

"The dog on the cot says otherwise."

"You're not sleeping on the cot, either," he pointed out. "Even if I hadn't given the other cot to that lady, I'll bet you would have let Casper sleep on yours."

She waved away his words. "That's being logical. All this travel has been hard enough on him."

"And you." Zoey had told him about her all-important task of crisscrossing the country so Casper could breed with a champion. So it had come to this: he envied a dog.

"I don't count," she said. "Casper has to feel well enough to make puppies, or this whole trip is for nothing."

He let the strands of her hair sift through his fingers. "He'll be fine. It takes more than a few sore muscles for an interested male to ignore a willing female."

"Is that so?"

"Absolutely." He looked at her. "Trust me." All the frustrated desire he felt for her was in those two words.

In the silence that followed, the atmosphere changed. He should say something to cut the tension, but he didn't. Couldn't.

Slowly, Zoey propped herself on her elbow again, her hair curtained behind her, her mouth mere inches away. "Does that apply to any male?"

Her voice was low and husky and Cam was pretty sure he heard willingness in it. That was all it took for hot desire to pulse through his body again. The cold ache in his hip disappeared—although it could have become numb—and he was definitely interested. Very interested. "Yeah."

She regarded him without blinking. Her lips were dark, stained by the Cherry Eruption. He hoped his weren't the sickening yellow green of the Lemon Lime Lightning. He ran his tongue over them.

Zoey's gaze dropped to his mouth and her hair rippled as she swayed a fraction of an inch closer.

Cam's interest grew. Caveman thoughts shoved common sense out of the way. *Want woman,* check. *Take woman to cave,* check. *Claim woman as mate,* still on the to-do list. Time to check that one off.

"What are you thinking?" she murmured.

"Oh…you don't wanna know."

"Oh…I kinda do."

Cam reached out and twisted a piece of her shiny hair around his finger. "I'm wondering what a disgustingly good person would do right now so I can do the opposite."

6

"THANK GOODNESS," ZOEY said without irony.

Her heart pounded with heavy, syrupy thuds. He was going to kiss her again. Finally.

Eyes on hers, Cam twirled his finger in her hair, drawing her inevitably closer. Even in the poor light, she could see the intensity in his eyes. Just before their lips locked together, Zoey wondered if he'd remember that they were in an airport terminal. Then his lips brushed hers before settling in, and Zoey wondered if *she'd* remember they were in an airport terminal.

Sensation fizzed from her lips through her body, and Zoey didn't *care* that they were in an airport terminal. Her stomach felt as though she'd swallowed a sparkler. Wow. Just wow.

And they were only kissing. Not touching any place but their lips. He released her hair and Zoey swore it tingled, although she knew that was impossible.

This was better than their previous kiss. She feathered her fingers against the roughness of his jaw, just in case he was thinking of going anywhere, and because she was balanced on her elbow—if she leaned closer, she was going to fall into him.

Cam must have been on her wavelength because his hand moved around to her shoulder and he fell back, pulling her with him.

Zoey gasped, breaking the kiss when she found herself splayed over his body. Automatically, she braced her arms on the floor to take some of the weight off him and her hair fell forward, covering his face.

Oh, no, not a sexy one-shouldered slide for her, just a clump of hair covering his eyes, nose and mouth.

She tried to shake it off him but only succeeded in whipping it against his face.

He chuckled and used both hands to brush it away. Still smiling, he slowly combed his fingers through the strands, spreading them out. Reaching around, he drew the rest of her hair forward.

His fingers brushed the back of her neck and her arms quivered in response. He must have noticed but kept slowly combing his fingers through her hair until it curtained their faces.

Inhaling, he murmured, "I've been dreaming about this, about you lying on top of me with your hair surrounding us, keeping out the world. Keeping out everything and everyone."

Something uncoiled deep within Zoey. A drugging warmth spread through her and her arms stopped trembling. "So it's not just me then," she breathed.

Cam splayed his hands over her shoulder blades and gently pressed until her elbows gave and she lay fully against him. "It's not just you then."

Even though her hair blocked out most of the light, she could see a faint reflection in his eyes as he studied her face, really looking at her in a way no one had in years. Zoey felt oddly exposed. What if he didn't like what he saw?

"Now what?" she whispered.

He grinned. "Now you kiss me."

"Oh." Zoey had been thinking more long term, more what-do-we-do-about-this-thing-between-us, but kissing him worked. "I can do that."

As she lowered her head, Zoey wondered if this was his fantasy or hers. Her eyes drifted shut only to blink open when she realized she'd never allowed herself to have this particular fantasy—not the whole fooling-around-in-public-while-stranded-in-an-airport thing, but the fantasy where she acted solely to please herself without deferring to her boyfriends' preferences. She'd pretended their preferences were her preferences. She'd faked it.

And that hadn't been fair to them or to her.

She couldn't fake it with Cam even if she wanted to because she didn't know what he liked, but she did know he wanted to learn what *she* liked. And so did she.

Not one, not a single one of her J boyfriends had ever… she swallowed against a sudden knot of tears in her throat.

Really? She was going to get all emotional *now,* when a hot guy was waiting for her to kiss him?

She was a mess.

"Zoey?" His fingers rubbed slow circles over her spine. "You okay?"

She nodded, her hair rippling. It *was* kind of cool having her hair around them. "I'm having a moment."

She brushed her fingers along his jaw to assure him it wasn't a *bad* moment.

He smiled slightly and kept gently caressing her back. He didn't pull her head toward his or talk to her in a get-over-yourself voice.

He waited. For her. It was her kiss and she could do whatever she wanted. And what she wanted was soft and slow with plenty of time to explore and learn.

With her J boyfriends, she'd had to steal those moments. They were always impatient with her—why had she tolerated it? Why had she allowed them to always decide what was sexy? Sure, fast could be hot and fun, but slow could be sensual and sweet. Hadn't she been worth the extra minutes?

She and Cam had all kinds of time and for once, Zoey was going to indulge herself.

"I like you, Cam."

"I like you, too, Zoey." His mouth moved as though he wanted to smile and tried to stop, then gave up and grinned. "Was that your moment?"

"Mmm." She leaned down and murmured next to his ear, "Because you gave me my moment, you'll be amply rewarded with a few moments of your own."

She pulled his earlobe into her mouth and gently ran her teeth over it.

He jerked, but she wasn't sure if it was from surprise or pleasure. She hesitated, then realized she was waiting for him to roll her over or start kissing her to speed things up because that's what her J boyfriends would have done.

Never again.

Deliberately, Zoey repeated the soft scrape of her teeth against Cam's earlobe and his breathing hitched. He liked it. And she might never have known. But now that she did… She flicked her tongue in the little hollow just beneath his ear and he made a soft sound. Earlobes, so underrated.

She moved down his jaw, planting soft kisses and inhaling his scent. It was there, underneath the faint aroma of avocado from her lotion and the industrial airport smell that clung to travelers.

Zoey was all about scents. She'd describe his as rich and round, healthy. Not the overly sweet, metallic odor of boyfriends who became couch potatoes, smoked and ate junk food.

Cam had stilled, his hands heavy on her back; he was waiting to see what she'd do next. She kissed his chin, his cheeks, his eyes. And she kissed the place where a dimple would be—if he were smiling. She teased the spot with her tongue, coaxing, and the corner of his mouth tilted upward, revealing the dimple.

Using her finger, Zoey traced the dip and moved across his lips.

They puckered in a kiss.

She glanced up to find him watching her. His hands started moving over her back again, and this time she noticed there was the slightest pressure. It was an encouragement more than a demand, but Zoey didn't need any encouragement.

She lowered her mouth to his, matching upper lip to upper lip and lower lip to lower lip. With exquisite slowness, she brushed them together, giving each little nerve ending a chance to wake up before she kissed him in earnest.

A sound escaped Cam's throat. Clutching her to him, he moved his legs from beneath hers and settled her between them.

There was no doubt that she'd turned him on. And there was no doubt she'd turned herself on. There had been an awareness humming between them for hours. It was a relief to finally act on it.

They traded long, deep kisses that fed Zoey's soul. People were always vaguely disappointed and irritated with her. Cam didn't kiss her as though he was disappointed or irritated. He kissed her as though he'd forgotten all about the beer mess she'd been responsible for.

Even better, he made her forget about it, too.

When was the last time she'd kissed a man for so long her lips had gone numb? Even the scrape of Cam's beard no longer registered. She was going to have one heck of a case of beard burn, but she had creams for that.

Zoey raised her head and looked down at Cam. His eyes remained closed, but he shifted beneath her. Now that she wasn't actively kissing him, Zoey noticed the cold seeping into her knees and the tips of her toes where they touched the floor beyond the skimpy blanket. And she'd been pressing Cam's entire body against the hard cold for ages.

"The floor has got to be uncomfortable for you."

Eyes still closed, he grinned and settled her more firmly against him. "What floor?"

Zoey laughed and kissed him again.

What had started as slow and sweet suddenly became hot and urgent.

Even as close as they were, she wanted to be closer, wanted to touch and be touched. Cam's breathing thundered in her ears as his hands moved up and down her body. Zoey couldn't stay still. She rocked against him, unable to stifle a long, frustrated moan.

She froze. What if someone heard? She wrenched her mouth from his and pushed up so she could see over Casper's crate and the luggage barricade into the hall.

Their panting breaths were so loud, they nearly echoed.

"Are we attracting an audience?" Cam asked.

Zoey waited, but no one walked past. "Not a human one."

Casper had opened his eyes partway, but as Zoey watched, he gave a doggy sigh and the lids slowly closed.

She and Cam looked at each other and snickered.

"It's late," Zoey said. "We should get some sleep, too."

But she didn't move and neither did Cam. Their breathing slowed and their smiles faded.

"Are you sleepy?" he asked.

Zoey shook her head as his hands traveled down her back and his fingers found the hem of her sweater. He pulled the tank she wore beneath it from her jeans and exposed a sliver of skin to the cold air.

That wasn't why she shivered.

Or why she tugged the layers he wore from his jeans and ran her hands up the sides of his rib cage.

He gasped. "Your fingers are cold!"

"You'll just have to warm them up," she murmured and laughed. "That sounded so cheesy."

"I don't care." And he unhooked her bra.

Zoey blinked. "Really?" She was questioning herself as much as Cam.

"I sure hope so." He gazed into her eyes as his fingers caressed her skin beneath the sweater and tank.

She was hyperaware of every little movement and those little movements felt very good. So good it was hard to think. Worse, she couldn't remember why she needed to think. "This…reminds me of high school."

"When you stole every opportunity to touch the other person and drive yourself crazy even though it couldn't go any farther?" He grinned. "Yeah, I know."

She grinned back. "I never dreamed I'd miss that."

"People are in too much of a hurry these days. I'm guilty, too. But right now I want to enjoy our journey without worrying about getting to the destination."

"You're not talking about Seattle."

"I'm not talking about Seattle."

Zoey drew a shuddering breath and lowered herself until her head rested on Cam's chest. She heard his heart beating, strong and steady, like the man himself.

And that was it. Her J boyfriends had been just that: boys. Cam was a man, and it made all the difference.

Zoey decided she liked men. Or at least this one. She tilted her head until her chin balanced on his chest and observed him as his fingers drew lazy circles against her skin.

"This is nice," he said, and Zoey hummed a little sigh of agreement before scooting close enough to his neck to nuzzle it.

Cam widened the circles and they weren't so lazy anymore. His heart still beat steadily, although it was a little faster and a little harder.

She smiled against his neck and moved her fingers along his ribs.

"Hey, that tickles."

"Nice tickles or bad tickles?"

"You tell me." And he skimmed his thumbs upward beneath her bra straps to where her breasts pillowed under her arms. He traced the side of the curves and then underneath as far as his thumbs could reach.

Zoey muffled a noise that sounded embarrassingly like a giggle and he immediately increased the pressure so it didn't tickle anymore. Far from it. She held her breath as he stroked back and forth. Back and forth.

Watching her. Waiting. Driving her crazy.

Zoey squirmed. Her nipples were tight and hard, and he had to be able to feel them, even through all the layers they wore.

She moved again, trying to give him access, but Cam suddenly gripped her hips and held them still. The hard bulge in his jeans pressed against her belly. It wasn't comfortable right there. But it would be more than comfortable pressed elsewhere—and she knew the exact spot. She tried to wiggle her way up Cam's body, but he held her in place, his breathing harsh.

"Time to take a break," he muttered.

What? "We just took a break," she protested.

"We need another one."

"Nooo," she groaned. "I don't want to."

"Neither do I, which is why we should."

Stalemate. Unless…could she really do it?

Yes. Yes, she could.

"You're not going to stop." Zoey raised herself off Cam's chest and wiggled her shoulders.

"Zoey…" His voice held a warning.

"Cam…" Her voice held an invitation.

The breath hissed between his teeth as he released her hips and covered her breasts with his hands.

"Yes," she whispered, relieved and wanting more at the same time.

She sucked her lip between her teeth and rocked her hips. Cam responded by flicking his thumbs across her nipples.

Zoey moaned and dropped her head back as she continued to rub against him.

"You feel so good," he whispered.

This was better than good. It was pretty great, actually. She moaned again and Cam did, too, although his moan sounded more like a whimper. Yeah. She knew how he felt. He whined and she wanted to whine, too, except then he growled.

Growled? They both stilled and turned their heads to find a grumpy Afghan hound staring at them.

Another growl sounded low in the dog's throat.

"Oh, hey…" For a second, she couldn't think of his name. "Casper, it's okay. I'm okay."

She swallowed and said to Cam, "I guess he's trying to protect me."

"Or me," Cam said.

Good point. It was obvious that Casper preferred Cam

to Zoey. And she was on top of Cam in a dominant position, so that might have something to do with it, too.

Slowly, Zoey eased off Cam and curled against his side.

Cam put his arm around her shoulders and drew her close. To the dog, he said, "Go back to sleep, buddy. It's all good."

Casper whined a couple more times before he laid his head down again.

"We'll see how he likes it when he gets all hot and bothered around Alexandra and I growl at *him*," Zoey grumbled.

Cam chuckled and kissed the top of her head. "Go to sleep, Zoey."

As if she could. She snuggled closer, burrowing her hand beneath his sweater and stroking his bare chest. He had a great chest. She stifled a yawn. Very manly. "Are you going to be able to sleep?"

"Not if you keep doing that."

She smiled and left her hand resting over his heart, feeling the beat grow slower....

"*How* many days?" Zoey looked stricken.

"They're scheduling flights two days out right now, but realistically, by the time we reach the ticket counter it could be three days or longer." Cam hated telling her that. They'd overslept, for which he blamed himself, but honestly, claiming a place in the long line a few hours earlier wouldn't have made that much of a difference.

For the past several hours, they'd taken turns standing in line and watching Casper and their luggage. People were okay with letting others leave briefly for food and restroom breaks, and a few enterprising kids hired themselves out as place holders for those who wanted a longer break.

Cam had just hired one so he could scout around before

trading line duty with Zoey—the incredibly sexy Zoey, who'd awakened in his arms just a few hours ago. Cam felt great, considering he'd slept on the floor and one of his arms had been numb. But Zoey had been with him, and watching her wake up and smile at him with those huge, sleepy, green eyes was better than any energy drink.

Those eyes were now filled with worry, and he was about to make it worse. "More bad news. Another storm is on the way. From the north this time. We may be stuck here even longer."

"You're kidding."

Cam shook his head. "The airport has equipment to deal with the snow, but the workers can't keep the runways clear because of the wind."

Zoey slumped against the wall. "I can't believe this is happening. I wasn't in charge. I didn't even book the tickets. All I had to do was get on the plane with the dog."

"Which you did. So stop beating yourself up." Cam spoke sharply on purpose. He didn't want Zoey to be distracted by undeserved guilt. "And don't let anyone else beat you up, either."

She blinked and saluted. "Yes, *sir*."

"That's more like it." He grinned at her and was relieved to see her attempt to smile back.

It wasn't much of a smile, but it was something. "We've got options. Instead of trying to fly directly to Seattle, we can ask to be routed to another airport and catch a flight to Seattle from there."

"I considered that," she told him. "But I wonder if going to another airport will get us to Seattle any faster." She looked down at Casper. "And I still have to be on a plane with a climate-controlled cargo hold."

Cam looked at Casper, too. "I don't know anything

about dog breeding. How long do we have before it's too late?"

"I have no idea, but from what Kate said, the window of opportunity is open for just a few days, and then it closes."

"I appreciate your use of euphemisms."

Zoey laughed. It was good to hear. "I'm even using them in my head!"

Cam laughed with her even though his own window of opportunity with Richard had slammed shut.

He hadn't told Zoey that his meeting was toast, and he wasn't going to. He'd already decided he wanted to do everything in his power to make sure Casper kept his date. Plus, he needed to spend time away from the brewery, and he wanted to spend it with Zoey.

But if she found out there was now no real reason for him to go to Seattle, she wouldn't let him help her. She'd already asked why he was visiting hops farms in January—something Richard hadn't questioned—and he'd admitted it was only so he could give Richard a reason why he was in the area.

"People are getting together and renting vans to drive to other airports," he said. "But I checked, and all the rental places are out of cars. They've posted signs with the number of people on the waiting list."

"Driving to another airport is not a bad idea. And more cars will come in as the roads clear." Zoey pushed herself off the wall. "My turn in line."

"I'm paying the kid by the hour, if you want to walk Casper. Or I can."

Zoey reached down and scratched Casper's head. "I'll walk him. I'd appreciate the fresh air. Come here, Casper." As she knelt to put on his coat, she said, "At some point, I'm going to have to take these bands out of his hair."

Her own hair slid forward, instantly reminding Cam of

last night. And early this morning. He swallowed as desire flared. It was always there now, humming along beneath the surface until moments such as this, when it was all he could do not to take her in his arms and finish what they'd started last night.

He had it bad for her. So bad. *It's why men make poor decisions with the wrong women.* Gus was only partially right this time. Men could just as easily make poor decisions with the right woman. Cam was going to have to be careful.

He inhaled deeply, trying to clear his head, when another of the unceasing airport announcements came on. Pausing as she put on Casper's bonnet, Zoey listened before saying ruefully, "I keep expecting them to call my name. I haven't turned on my phone this morning, and knowing Kate, she'll have me paged if I don't check in soon."

"Wouldn't it be better to call her and get it over with?" Cam asked.

Zoey stood and slipped on her coat. "And tell her what?"

"Tell her if she pages you, you'll lose your place in line."

"Ooh, you're good." She flashed him a grin and he got a little lost in her eyes.

There was a word for how he was feeling. Besotted.

"There you are!" A motorized scooter rolled to a stop beside them, driven by an older woman with a bandaged foot. "I called to you by the car rentals, but you didn't hear me. You very kindly gave me your cot last night," she explained when Cam couldn't get his brain working fast enough to figure out who she was.

"Right." A lot had happened since last night. Cam forced himself to refocus. "I recognize the foot. How is it this morning?"

She grimaced. "It might be broken but it's too swollen

to be sure. Luckily, the airport located an orthopedist, so I do have some medical advice and pain meds. I wanted to thank you again for giving me your cot, but that's not why I followed you. Were you trying to rent a car?"

Cam glanced at Zoey. "We were considering it."

"As it happens, I have a rental, but I can't drive." She gestured to her foot. "I was meeting my grandson here so we could drive together to his sister's—my granddaughter's—wedding. But his flight was canceled and he's driving directly from Philadelphia. The wedding is this afternoon, and I don't want anyone in the family to risk making a trip from Rochelle to pick me up, so..." She looked at Cam. "I wondered if you would agree to drive me to the wedding, and then you can have the car."

It could be the solution to their problems—or it could create more problems. "That's very generous, considering you don't even know me—us," Cam said, with a glance at Zoey. They should discuss this.

"I'm Joyce," the woman said. Then she laughed. "And you're Cameron MacNeil. You own a brewery in Texas and are somehow connected to a kennel in Virginia."

"How do you know all that?" Zoey asked her.

She pointed to Casper's crate, which sported the kennel's name; the box of beer with the MacNeil's logo and the luggage tag on Cam's suitcase. "And my grandson Googled you."

Cam was torn between admiration at Joyce's resourcefulness and being unnerved that it had been so easy to learn his identity.

"What do you think, Zoey?"

Zoey clutched his arm and pulled him away. "It's not part of the plan."

"Call your sister and tell her the plan's changed."

"She won't like it." But she was already switching on

her cell phone. "I'm not sure I'll be able to reach them unless they're in their room. They don't have cell reception at the resort."

"We should take Joyce up on her offer," Cam said. "We might not get another opportunity."

Zoey squeezed her eyes shut. "This always happens to me. I go off plan to take advantage of an opportunity and it ends up being a mistake. Every. Single. Time."

"Zoey, listen to me."

She opened her eyes.

"Your goal is not to get on a plane. Your goal is to get Casper to the kennel. Your sister's plan didn't cover blizzards. You need a new plan. Sticking with the old one is a mistake."

Her phone warbled its readiness and Zoey punched in a number. Cam signaled to Joyce that they'd be just a few more minutes. Zoey covered one ear with her hand and pressed her phone tightly against the other ear.

Cam held her gaze until she slowly lowered the phone and turned it off. She glanced at Casper, then to the end of the corridor, where crowds of people walked back and forth.

She stepped toward Joyce and held out her hand. "I'm Zoey," she said. "And we're incredibly grateful."

"So do we have a deal?" Joyce asked.

Cam looked at Zoey and she nodded. "Deal," they said at the same time.

7

WHAT WOULD HAVE taken just over an hour in normal conditions took nearly five hours. The drive seemed even longer because Casper had to ride in his crate to make room in the rear seat.

Zoey could hear him licking his paws because she'd forgotten to spray them with bitter apple. And he seemed to have figured out that Joyce was to blame for him riding in the crate because he growled whenever she edged too close.

Zoey should have ridden in the back with him, but she'd thought Joyce would be more comfortable there as she was able to prop up her foot. By the time Zoey realized she'd made a mistake, it was too late. Between Joyce's foot, the heavy, slow-moving traffic and the deep piles of snow on either side of the highway, there was no easy way to stop and switch.

Joyce was a talker. Zoey had her own moments of babbling, but Joyce was a pro. She told them all about her family's tradition of being married on January twenty-first, St. Agnes Day, which explained why the wedding was in the middle of the week.

Then she weaseled all sorts of information out of Zoey and Cam and gave them advice. She was absolutely right when she told Cam that if his family wanted a say in how the brewery was run, then they should be doing more of the work required to run it. But she was all wrong when she advised Zoey to stop being afraid of failure and get a real job.

"I'm not afraid of failure," Zoey replied. "In fact, I'm very familiar with it." Zoey explained about her Skin Garden creams and even gave Joyce her lemon-and-olive travel balm.

Joyce squinted at the jar with the specially-printed label, unscrewed the lid and sniffed. "What's your business plan?" She smeared some of the balm onto her hands.

Conscious of Cam sitting next to her, Zoey said, "It's too early for that yet."

Sighing heavily, Joyce shook her head. Of course, Joyce *would* be a retired high school vocational business teacher. "You're afraid. You're afraid to try too hard because you might fail. When you commit to a business plan, you're all in, you're putting your heart into it and success or failure is all on you. Without a plan, when you fail—and you will— it's easier to convince yourself it doesn't count because it wasn't as though you were seriously trying." Joyce paused. "It doesn't hurt as much that way."

Zoey's face heated. "I plan." She didn't dare look at Cam. "But my plans always go wrong."

"Make better plans," Joyce said from the backseat. "That goes for you, too," she warned Cam.

"I have a business model," Cam said mildly.

"But it doesn't do any good if you don't follow it."

How could Joyce be one-hundred-percent right about Cam and one-hundred-percent wrong about Zoey? *Because she's not,* said a little voice that Zoey tried so very hard not to hear.

But she did hear, and it made her very grumpy.

"It's not that I don't have a business plan," Zoey said, not wanting to sound like a total incompetent in front of Cam. "It's that I don't have the resources to implement it." Listen to those words. Didn't that sound professional?

"And how do you plan to acquire those resources?"

"Working and saving." And avoiding expensive mistakes.

Joyce shot more questions at her. "Exactly how much financing do you need? How long will it take to acquire? Are there alternate sources of revenue? Potential investors?"

"I—"

"That's part of a business plan, too." Joyce shifted in the seat as she reached for her purse.

Casper hummed a throaty warning as her foot moved closer to his travel kennel. It was a pre-growl. Zoey wondered if he used it at dog shows to warn other dogs without being heard by the judges.

"In fact, we can brainstorm one for you right now." From her purse, Joyce withdrew a small leather-covered notebook and shifted away from Casper. "If I were still teaching, we'd be gearing up for the Starting a Small Business unit. I've helped hundreds of students formulate business plans over the years. It was my favorite part of the curriculum." She exhaled heavily. "I really miss it. They say that when you retire you can do all those things you've always wanted to do, but you know what? Watching students learn to start a business and then have some of those businesses become reality? That's what I loved. So this will be such a treat for me. And after we hash out a plan for Zoey, we can fix Cam's."

At that, Zoey's eyes widened and she glanced at him. Through it all, he'd remained outwardly calm, and although Zoey had seen his knuckles occasionally go white where he gripped the steering wheel, he'd never complained or lost his temper. He'd even politely answered a few of Joyce's questions. Considering he had a degree in business and actually had started his own company, Zoey was in awe of his restraint.

But this might send him over the edge. To spare him, Zoey kept Joyce's focus on her the rest of the way to Rochelle. Joyce asked questions that Zoey couldn't answer, and even more questions Zoey didn't *want* to answer, especially with Cam listening in.

"Who is your target market?" Joyce asked a few hours later, holding up the jar.

"People with skin," Zoey answered. She was a little snappish at this point.

"Young skin? Old skin? Dry skin? Damaged skin? Ethnic skin? Sensitive skin? Irritated skin? Male skin? Female skin?" Joyce was relentless.

"I'm still researching." That had become Zoey's default answer.

By the time they reached the city limits of Rochelle, Zoey felt defensive and incompetent.

"I will say that packaging your samples in generic, gender-neutral jars was an excellent decision while you're still testing," Joyce said.

"Thanks." Zoey managed a smile, even though she hadn't thought they were either generic or gender neutral. But Joyce had obviously wanted to end with a positive comment, even though it was actually another negative. "You've given me a lot to consider," she added.

Joyce tore many tiny pages out of her notepad and handed them to her. "After you've had a chance to finalize a plan, send it to me and I'll review it for you. I wrote my email address on one of the pages."

Just as Zoey was about to politely decline, Cam said, "That's a very generous offer. You should take her up on it, Zoey." He didn't add, "You need all the help you can get." But to Zoey, it was implied.

She was deluding herself if she believed she would ever be a success at anything, and now Cam probably believed it, too. That stung.

Cam drove Joyce directly to the church, where the family had delayed the wedding for nearly an hour. Her grandson arrived just as they were saying goodbye, and Cam and Zoey drove off to the sight of an exuberant family reunion. Seeing how happy they were and how jubilantly they all waved at her and Cam, Zoey forgot her embarrassment at having her business incompetence exposed.

With a sigh, she settled into the front seat. Casper had been freed from his crate and was gnawing on an "emergency only" chew toy. They were emergency only because apparently he became overly attached to them. Phyllis from the kennel hadn't explained exactly what "overly attached" entailed. At this point, Zoey didn't care.

"We did a good deed and nothing went wrong," she said to Cam. He'd been awfully quiet, and she suspected it was not just because she and Joyce had done all the talking.

Cam leaned forward and surveyed the sky through the windshield. "Mmm."

"What do you mean, 'mmm'? I don't like the sound of 'mmm.'"

"The sky looks…heavy."

"You mean like snow heavy?" Zoey peered outside. The clouds were gray, but they were always gray in winter, weren't they? Besides, it was already dusk and the streetlights were starting to come on.

"I'm not familiar with snow clouds, but if we were back in Texas, I'd say we were in for a frog strangler," Cam said. "Since we're in the north and it's cold, I'm guessing snow and lots of it."

"But the new storm isn't supposed to start for another day." The tree branches were still frosted with yesterday's white stuff.

"I suppose you can try reasoning with it." That was uncharacteristically sarcastic for Cam.

Zoey studied him. The strain showed on his face as he inched the car down freshly plowed streets. Neither one of them had much experience with snowy road conditions, and so far, Cam had done all the driving. "You must be exhausted. I should be driving. I'm sorry. We could have switched at the church, but it didn't occur to me."

"I'm fine." Cam didn't sound fine. "But we should get something to eat and figure out a plan."

"A plan. Right. Clearly, you're on your own there."

He smiled. "Joyce was rough on you. Not that she wasn't right, but it's a lot to take in all at once. And she's not as familiar with internet-based businesses. The rules are different."

"You're being very kind." Because that's the type of guy he was, she'd learned. "But I'm still embarrassed that you heard how unprepared I am."

"Hey. You took one for the team so I could concentrate on the road. I appreciate that."

They stopped at a red light and Cam sent a dazzler of a smile her way. With dimples.

That smile and the warmth in his eyes made her feel a whole lot better. She even managed to return his smile. As they gazed at each other, awareness prickled to life. With Joyce in the car, Zoey had been able to ignore the tug of attraction, but Joyce wasn't in the car now. She knew the moment Cam had the same thought because the intensity returned to his eyes along with something else. It took a few seconds before Zoey recognized the expression as the same one she'd seen on dieting girlfriends when faced with a cupcake. Hunger. Desire. And the struggle with temptation.

Cam was staring at her as though she was a cupcake. He didn't glance away until the light changed.

The only sound in the car was Casper biting his chew toy. "So where are we going?" Zoey asked to break the silence.

Cam shook his head. "I'm not sure, but wherever we're headed, it's going to take a while to get there."

They stopped at a fast-food place that had Wi-Fi. Cam sat inside with his laptop and Zoey walked Casper around the snowy parking lot. Dogs weren't allowed inside unless they were service dogs. Show dogs, even those who wore outfits that had their name embroidered on it, didn't count. Zoey tried demonstrating Casper's judging pose, but the teenaged manager on duty hadn't been impressed.

So Cam sat in a booth by the window and they shouted through it as they decided what to do next.

Zoey marched around outside on frozen feet. She was wearing boots, but poor Casper wasn't. He didn't seem bothered and took his time sniffing at the lumps of snow-covered bushes lining the sidewalk. She could have left him in the car and gone inside with Cam, but given her luck, the car would have been stolen with Casper inside.

Besides, she enjoyed watching Cam. It was dark outside now and if she stayed beyond the pool of landscape lighting, he couldn't see her from inside the brightly lit restaurant.

He hadn't shaved, so he had that sexy stubble thing going on. She and Casper had circled the building and were now approaching Cam head on. His face was tinged blue from the reflection of the laptop screen and he stared with an intensity that gave him a sinister sexiness.

He started typing, which drew her attention to his

hands. She remembered the feel of those hands on her bare skin, and her knees went a little weak.

He'd made her forget they were in an airport terminal. He'd made her forget *everything* except his touch. She'd wanted more and more, and if Casper hadn't growled...

Zoey looked down at the dog and caught him pawing at something in the shrubs. Then he dropped his head to eat whatever he'd found and Zoey jerked his leash.

"Casper, no!" Kate had stressed that he absolutely, positively was never to eat anything except his very own special food. Not one mouthful.

When he pulled against the leash, Zoey tried to distract him. "Casper, let's see what Cam's found."

Cam had been typing rapidly for several minutes and Zoey stepped close to the window to try and make out what was on the computer screen. But before she could, Cam closed the laptop, grabbed the bag of extra fast food and hurried toward the door.

"Let's go." He pointed to the car. "I found a flight."

Zoey started after him, but Casper barked and sat down on the sidewalk.

"Casper, come on!" Zoey tugged the leash and Casper got up but pulled in the other direction.

"Casper!"

He whined.

"There is no way you have to go again, and if you do, you're just going to have to hold it."

"Zoey! Come on!" Cam waved to her from inside the car, which he'd already started.

"Sorry, Casper." Zoey grabbed his collar and half-dragged him across the parking lot. He whined pitifully and wouldn't jump inside. When she picked him up, or tried to, he fought her. Cam finally had to come around and help her get the dog into the car.

Then Casper tried to jump into the front seat and escape, so Zoey sat in the rear with him and attempted to calm him down.

"What's his problem?" Cam asked as Casper whined frantically and scratched at the windows.

"I have no idea. I've never seen him act like this." Then again, she hadn't been around Casper all that much.

Cam studied him in the rearview mirror. "Maybe he saw some animal. A cat or maybe another dog."

"I didn't see anything, and he didn't go this crazy when we were walking outside. Besides, he's around strange dogs at shows all the time."

Casper barked and Cam flinched. If the guy didn't lose his temper after putting up with this, he was definitely a keeper.

Zoey finally got Casper to sit and attempted to attach his special seat belt harness, but while she was bent over, Casper scrambled across her back, his nails digging into her.

"Ow! Casper!"

Casper propped himself against the door and stared out the window, whining and panting. The car smelled like wet dog and French fries.

Zoey tried to remove his coat, but that set him off again. He frantically scrambled over her lap from one side of the car to the other. "Down, Casper!" She tried a few commands in the calm, firm tone Phyllis had taught her to use, but the further they traveled away from the restaurant, the more agitated the dog became.

Twenty minutes later, they reached the final intersection before they'd have to merge onto the interstate. Once the car stopped, though, Casper started barking again, high-pitched yips that made Zoey's ears ring.

This wasn't working. She met Cam's eyes in the rearview mirror. Without a word, he turned the car around and headed back to the fast-food place.

"I'm sorry," Zoey said, not sure if Cam heard her over Casper's yipping.

The dog quieted when she put his leash on, as though he sensed they were going back.

"What flight did you find?" Zoey was almost afraid to ask. Cam had been in such a hurry.

"A six a.m. flight from Des Moines."

"*Des Moines?* As in Iowa?"

He nodded. "There was nothing in Kansas City or St. Louis, and all the nearby regional airports route through O'Hare. Another problem I ran into is that many commuter planes can't take Casper's big kennel. This Des Moines flight uses larger planes on both legs of the flight. It stops in Denver and then we'll be in Seattle by ten-thirty tomorrow morning."

Zoey exhaled. They'd be pulling an all-nighter, but it was much better than sleeping, or trying to sleep, in an airport terminal for another couple of days. "But Iowa—how long of a drive are we talking about?"

He checked the dashboard. "The GPS estimates four hours. Under normal conditions. Realistically, we should tack on at least another hour. Maybe two."

The clock in the car said it was currently after seventhirty. Zoey counted the hours off on her fingers. The best-case scenario had them at the airport by midnight or 1:00 a.m., depending on when they stopped going backward. They'd have to be there no later than four to check Casper in. Even with this little hiccup, they had a threehour cushion.

This could work. Would work. Zoey allowed herself to relax.

Neither spoke on the return drive to the fast-food place.

After parking, Zoey opened the door and Casper bolted out, dragging her toward the shrubbery that lined the outside of the restaurant. There, he nosed around, sniffing and pawing at the ground.

"How can he smell anything through the snow?" Cam stood beside her as they both watched Casper and let him lead them around the building.

"He's a dog," Zoey said. Her keychain had a tiny light on it and she shined it at the bushes. If Casper found whatever he was searching for, Zoey wanted a heads up.

Out of the corner of her eye, she saw Cam check his watch. Once. After that, he kept his hands shoved into his pockets and didn't complain. But he didn't speak.

Zoey couldn't stand it. "You could swear or something," she said.

"I am swearing. On the inside." He grinned. "Cussing out loud is not a good habit to fall into when you deal with the public. So I have a mental list of substitutes. I don't need to say them anymore. I just think of their number."

"Oh, so when you go all quiet, you're secretly swearing?"

He went all quiet and stared at her for a long moment. "Not all the time," he said softly.

"What's number one?"

"Darn."

"That's not bad. You could say darn in public."

He shook his head. "That's for when I shouldn't say anything."

"Oh. And what's number ten?"

"Why do you assume I have ten?"

"I'll bet you have more than ten. So what is it?"

He gave her a look. "A compound variation featuring number six with number seven used as an adjective."

"And what's this situation?"

"A one with potential." He pointed at Casper, who was lying on the sidewalk. "He's got something."

And she hadn't even noticed. Inhaling sharply, Zoey knelt, steeling herself to wrestle something nasty away from the dog. "It's what's left of the chew toy I gave him." She stood. "He must have carried it out of the car and dropped it. They warned me at the kennel that he becomes overly attached to them."

Cam raised his eyebrows. "Do you have any more of those?"

Zoey shook her head. "Come on, Casper."

The dog got up immediately, trotted to the car beside them and obediently jumped into the backseat. He settled himself and resumed gnawing at the misshapen lump. He didn't even protest when Zoey worked his hat off him.

Cam peered in at them. "Will you be okay here for a few minutes?"

She nodded and he took his laptop back inside the restaurant.

By the time he reappeared, bearing coffee and hot chocolate, Zoey had Casper's coat off and was attempting to dry his feet with paper towels. Casper wasn't fond of having his feet touched.

Cam set the cardboard drink holder on the front seat and started the car. "I found a pet store in DeKalb so we can get more of those magic chew toys."

"That's okay. I can buy them in Seattle."

"It's not just the chew toy. His coat is wet and I noticed you didn't bother with the booties. You can buy him something cheap but dry to wear."

"There's another coat in the suitcase, but I was saving it for Seattle. I want him to make a good impression." Which sounded silly now that Casper's paws were so dirty. Maybe she could clean them while they waited at the airport.

"So what will he wear on the plane?"

Zoey made a face. "You're right. I just hate that we're causing you all this trouble."

"Technically, Casper is causing the trouble, but I don't mind. You know why?"

"Because you're too busy going over your swear list?"

"Because if it weren't for Casper, I wouldn't have met you." His eyes caught hers in the rearview mirror.

"Oh." Her throat tightened so she couldn't joke about how his life would be easier. She swallowed hard and looked away, fiddling with her seat belt. "When you put it that way…" Reaching out, she scratched Casper's top-knot and mouthed, "Thank you" at him.

"Just don't expect anything from the designer rack," she murmured aloud. Then Cam's earlier comment sunk in. "Wait—you said DeKalb. That's in the wrong direction."

"PetWorld is the nearest store that stays open until nine." He merged onto the highway and Zoey read the mileage sign.

"Seventeen miles! Cam, are you sure you want to do this? Do we even have the time to do this?" As she asked, Zoey mentally subtracted from the previously comfortable cushion.

"We'll be fine," he assured her. "And we won't have to hang around the airport for as long."

"Excellent point."

In fact, they made great time. Zoey called her sister from the pet supply store and Kate even managed to calm down long enough to help Zoey choose approved items for Casper—except for the raincoat and booties. Casper's normal brand was only available online, and the only raincoat the store had in his size—that didn't strain Zoey's credit card too much—was in a zebra print with hot pink piping that said *Princess* on the side and had a blinged-out crown over the *i*. It came with matching booties. Kate would have been horrified, but it made both Zoey and Cam snicker—right up until they stepped outside and were smacked in the face by big, fat snowflakes.

8

We made it to Des Moines and I've turned in the car. You'll get a confirmation email. Great to meet you, and thanks again, Joyce.

CAM SENT THE TEXT and stopped by a men's room to change shirts and clean up. Because it was 4:00 a.m., the place was deserted, so he was even able to shave.

Other than his neck being a little stiff, he actually felt pretty good. But then, he'd slept for the past six hours while Zoey drove them all the way to the airport.

She'd only been able to convince him to let her drive because she pointed out that her sleep schedule was still messed up after working nights for several months. Cam had intended to doze for an hour or two at most, but when he woke up, they were in Des Moines and Zoey was looking a little ragged around the edges. He hoped she could sleep on the plane, but until then, he'd take care of her.

Cam liked the idea of that, which was a dangerous path to go down, but he wasn't concerned at the moment. He rubbed some of her skin balm into his skin, telling himself it was just because she'd asked for male input, but the truth was that it was wickedly cold outside and the balm kept his skin from hurting. So, yeah, he'd give it a thumbs up.

And, okay, the lemony scent reminded him of her. Not that he needed the reminder.

Cam was in a good mood—no, a great mood. It was amazing how sleep could change a person's outlook. He zipped up his bag and headed to the ticketing area. Zoey ought to be finished dealing with Casper's paperwork by now.

He smiled, remembering his emails with Gus. When he'd relayed to his cousin that they were driving to Des Moines, Gus had asked if the cold had frozen his brain. In reply, Cam had sent him a picture of Zoey and Casper that he'd taken with his phone. Gus had advised him to cool off one head and warm up the other.

Cam was still grinning as he made his way to the ticketing area—at least until he spotted a still figure in a candy-cane-striped hooded scarf sitting on a bench, clutching her cell phone and staring blindly into the distance. Casper's travel kennel and Cam's box were on the floor at her feet.

This was going to be bad.

Zoey didn't move when Cam sat beside her. Definitely bad. He waited for several moments before finally saying, "You don't act like a person who is about to get on a plane to Denver."

"Because I'm not a person who is about to get on a plane to Denver," she said quietly.

"What happened?" He twisted around and checked the empty ticket counter. "Don't tell me they sold out." Last night, there had been plenty of seats.

She shook her head and he noticed the phone she held. "Did the, uh, window close? Is it too late for Casper?"

"It's too cold for Casper. The airline won't let him on the plane if the temperature is below twenty degrees."

"But don't you have a waiver from the vet?" She had all kinds of papers. Cam had no idea traveling with dogs was such a hassle.

"All bets are off when it's below twenty degrees. It's nine degrees outside right now and the forecast says it won't get above sixteen today. Or tomorrow. Possibly even the day after. So Casper and I are stuck here until the next heat wave comes along."

Zoey spoke like a zombie and Cam realized she'd reached her limit. He'd been there. "I was focused on finding the right type of planes and a long-enough layover." He'd congratulated himself for discovering that not all commuter planes could accommodate Casper's large kennel. "I didn't read the rules about the temperature. I'm sorry."

"So am I. It was a mistake to leave Chicago."

"No, it's a mistake to give up."

She slumped. "Cam, right now, I'm so tired, all I want is to find a dog-friendly hotel so I can crash. And I'm not waking up until spring."

"Sounds like a plan. But I can come up with a better one."

Zoey managed a smile. "Funny thing about plans, they just never seem to go my way."

Cam let his gaze roam over her face. "That's not always a bad thing."

Her smile brightened and she quickly moved in to kiss him.

Cam knew she intended it to be a fast kiss, but he cupped the back of her head. Holding her in place, he deepened the kiss, just to reinforce that there were benefits to *some* plans going wrong.

"Hmm." She pulled away and this time, he let her go. "A good thing for us is still a bad thing for Casper."

They both peered into the crate, where Casper lay curled on his side, sleeping.

Zoey slumped down on the bench and sighed. "You'd better go buy your ticket."

No way. "I'm not getting on the plane without you."

"What about your meeting?"

"Richard can't meet with me today." Which was the truth. "So I can stick around."

"Cam, I'm not even sure I'm still taking Casper to Seattle. I'm waiting for Kate to call and tell me what to do."

"Then I'll wait with you."

"Will you at least get your ticket first?" She gestured behind him. "Better hurry. A crowd's forming."

Cam observed a single passenger at the counter.

"Very funny. Seriously, I don't have to be on that flight, and I'm not leaving you here on your own."

Her mouth flattened. "Why? Because I'm so clearly incompetent?"

"No. Because we're a team. No man—or woman, or dog—left behind."

She started to protest, but then her face softened.

Cam gazed into sea-green eyes swimming with emotion and felt himself completely fall for her. To be honest, it was more of a jump. Right off the cliff. The realization sent a tremor through him. Too fast. Too soon. He reminded himself they'd met in unusual circumstances and had bonded over shared inconvenience. This wasn't real life. It was the equivalent of a summer fling—or maybe not, since this was more of a winter-travel horror tale. They were both experienced enough to appreciate that fast-growing relationships had shallow roots. When they returned to their real lives, these intense feelings would evaporate.

Cam's voice of reason finished the lecture only to be

drowned out in a wave of desire. And he made sure Zoey saw that need in his eyes.

The longing in her expression changed to regret, and when she spoke, he noted resignation and a touch of bitterness in her voice. "You'd better escape while you can or I'll take you down with me."

He reached for her. "Zoey…you're saying that because you're tired—"

"I *know* I'm tired! That doesn't mean I'm not right." Sucking the breath between her teeth, she rubbed at her forehead and temples with both hands. Cam moved to take her in his arms, but her phone buzzed and chirped.

"It's Kate. I figured she'd be awake." She waved him off. "Go. Get your ticket. I'll be fine."

Cam hesitated, but she pulled away and turned her shoulder to him, so he stood and walked to the counter. He hoped she would be distracted by talking with her sister and not notice he'd left the box behind. If she spotted it, she'd realize that if he had any intention of getting on the flight, he would have taken it with him.

Dawn hadn't broken yet, but two more passengers had arrived and the airport was beginning to wake up. He heard a grinding sound as the employee of a coffee kiosk raised the metal grate and, thankfully, opened shop.

Cam waited all of a minute in line before it was his turn to talk to a ticket agent. "My friend and I are trying to transport a large dog to Seattle. She said something about a twenty-degree rule?"

He'd hoped to figure out a way around it, but after the agent explained, he realized that wasn't happening. "What about Denver? If we drove to Denver, what would be our chances of getting on a flight?" Cam wasn't sure how far it was to Denver. Or the temperature there. But he was sure that he wasn't leaving Zoey to hole up in Des Moines for days.

The agent pointed out several possibilities and suggested they stick to flights in the middle of the day. She offered to book tickets, but with the way their luck had been running, Cam decided to wait.

He headed back and found Zoey hunched over, face in her hand, still on the phone with her sister, so he kept walking past her all the way to the rental cars, where he proceeded to rent the biggest SUV available. Technically, the agencies weren't open yet. Technically, Cam didn't care. He stared at the one employee in the whole place until the guy switched on a computer.

As Cam signed the paperwork, he tried to figure out how he was going to convince Zoey that this was a good idea. Or plan, since she was all about following plans.

The rental agent had said that, depending on road conditions, Denver was about a nine-hour drive, which would put them there by mid-afternoon. If he and Zoey lucked into a flight today, they'd sleep in Seattle tonight, which had a familiar ring to it, or spend the night in Denver and fly out the next morning.

Lots of options. Abandoning Zoey was not one of them and he wasn't going to argue with her about it. He'd slept. She was exhausted. He'd wait until she passed out and carry her into the car if he had to.

Zoey was off the phone when Cam returned. "All set?" She stood and hoisted her backpack over her shoulder.

He nodded. "So are you headed for Seattle or going home?" It didn't matter to him because either way, she couldn't travel by air from Des Moines.

"Good news or, rather, not horrible news. We'll be okay if Casper gets to Merriweather Kennels within three days. Kate says Martha—she's the owner—is nervous and has lined up another stud but would really rather breed Alexandra to Casper." She looked down at the crate, where the dog had lifted his head when he heard his name. "I should redo his coat before she sees him, or she'll think he isn't worth the wait."

"Maybe she won't have to wait very long." Cam held up the key ring, the paper ID tag dangling.

Other than a couple of blinks, Zoey didn't react. She must be *really* tired.

"I rented an SUV," he explained.

"But…I don't want an SUV."

"I do. There'll be plenty of room for Casper. On the way to Denver," he added when she still said nothing.

"I'm not driving to Denver."

"No, I am. You'll be sleeping." Cam actually braced himself, expecting her to fling herself at him in exhausted gratitude.

She blinked a few more times and then exploded. "Are you *insane?*"

Not the reaction he was going for, but maybe a valid question. "Insane would be to hang around here, gambling that it'll be warm enough to fly out on Friday. Saturday morning is day three, Zoey." He held up three fingers. "You want to cut it that close?"

Stepping forward until she was right in his face, she tilted her chin. "It's insane for you to drive me to Denver when you're supposed to be flying to Seattle!"

So Zoey was both belligerent *and* irrational when she was tired. Duly noted. "It was my idea to leave Chicago, so it's my responsibility to get you to Denver."

"But what about your meeting with that Richard guy?"

"I'll catch a flight from Denver." Why was she arguing when she should have collapsed against him in gratitude by now?

"No, you're going to catch your flight here." She pointed to the security screening. "Now go!"

He did not go. For one thing, he didn't have a ticket. He had a car—a great, big gas guzzler of a car. "Do you honestly expect me to leave you? Is that the sort of guy you think I am? One who abandons his…friends when they need help?"

"I think you're the kind of guy who has an overdeveloped sense of responsibility. And when I say overdeveloped, I'm talking on steroids!"

"If the situation were reversed, would you get on the plane?"

"In a heartbeat!"

That stopped him momentarily. "No, you wouldn't. You're just saying that."

"We'll be going our separate ways when we get to Seattle anyway," Zoey pointed out. "And in that scenario, I would remind myself that you're only some guy I just met with a dog that's not even his. And I've got that meeting. That important meeting. You know, with an investor who'll *save my beer company*."

"Richard is not *saving* the brewery. The brewery is just fine." Cam wanted to make that clear. "Anyway, wouldn't you worry about me? I'm exhausted and…I have a dog."

"That's what cell phones are for!"

"A lot of good that does when I'm thousands of miles away!"

"Hey, there, you two. It's your lucky day." The barista from the coffee kiosk held a cardboard tray with two giant to-go cups. "You've won free coffee." He handed a cup to Zoey. "Take it with cream and sugar? Doesn't matter—you do today." He handed the other cup to Cam and backed away. "Drink up." He gestured with a little bow. "Enjoy."

Zoey was already chugging the coffee. As Cam took a

sip, he became aware of people staring at them. The place was actually getting crowded with business travelers arriving to catch the first flights of the day.

He and Zoey must have been arguing pretty loud. Now that they weren't yelling at each other, he could hear Casper whining. "Hey, buddy, it's okay." Cam held up the cup in thanks to the retreating barista and pressed on Zoey's shoulder until she sat down with him.

"Oh, that's just perfect." She drank deeply and Cam wondered how she didn't burn her tongue.

He generally took his coffee black, but the barista was right; the sweet, milky mixture was exactly what they both needed.

"I'm sorry," Zoey said when she came up for air. "I appreciate what you're trying to do, but what if something happens on the way to Denver? I would feel a lot better knowing you'd made it to Seattle in time to get a whole night's sleep before your meeting."

"I'd feel too guilty about abandoning you to sleep."

"Cam. I'm warning you, it's a mistake to stick with me."

"I disagree."

She shook her head and drained her coffee. Cam pried off the top of their cups and poured half his coffee into hers.

"Thanks."

As she drank that, Casper barked.

"Do you want coffee, too?" Cam asked him.

In response, Casper whined.

"He probably wants some water." Tossing her cup into the trash canister, Zoey got up, got water from her backpack and poured a tiny amount into the bowl attached to the kennel.

Casper sniffed at it and peered at her inquiringly. "It's not time for food," Zoey said.

Casper barked.

"Fine. Whatever." Kneeling, she dispensed a few bits into the other bowl.

"Why are you such a pushover for him and not for me?" Cam asked.

Zoey leaned her forehead against the crate and sighed. When she didn't answer, Cam realized that in spite of the coffee, she was falling asleep right there.

"Come on, Zoey." He shook her shoulder. "Let's go to Denver."

"Cam," she protested as he hauled her to her feet.

"You'll sleep in the car and when you wake up, you'll be in another city. Trust me—it's magical."

She gave him a tired smile as he pushed the luggage cart toward the ground transportation exit. "Why are you doing this?"

She wasn't following him and had that stubborn tilt to her chin that he'd only recently noticed. Abandoning the cart, he took her in his arms, leaned her back and kissed her. Hard. Long. And thoroughly. An old-fashioned, staking-a-claim movie kiss. Then he set her upright. "That's why."

WHEN ZOEY WOKE UP, the car wasn't moving. A vast expanse of white stretched outside the window, broken up occasionally by chain stores and fast-food places. Not so magical. "Where are we?"

It took a moment for the silence to register and for Zoey to realize that she was alone in the car. She wiped the condensation from the glass and was briefly disoriented because the car was in the same fast-food chain parking lot where Casper had lost his chew toy yesterday.

Either she was dreaming, or Cam was a creature of habit. Mental note: creature of habit.

She couldn't see him or Casper. Feeling groggy, she opened the car door and was blasted by frigid air.

Wow. Forcing herself to stand and slam the door shut, she rubbed at her arms and picked her way through gray slushy puddles across the parking lot to the restaurant entrance.

As she reached for the door, Cam and Casper came around the side. Cam was running, or trying to, and Casper was sticking to his show-dog gait. Zoey smiled as she watched them approach.

Cam answered her smile and slowed. "Hey."

"Hey yourself." She rubbed her arms, wishing she'd put on her coat. "Where are we?"

"Nebraska. Kearney, to be exact."

"Denver's not in Nebraska."

"Not much else is, either." Cam gestured to the door. "If you're hungry or anything, take advantage now. I'm trying to wear out Casper. He's been restless."

Casper barked.

Zoey reached down to pat his head, but he growled at her. Truly surprised, she jerked her hand away and tried to remember what command she should use, but settled for, "Casper! That's a major no-no," said in a very firm voice, or as firm as she could speak while shivering. "We'll discuss this later," she informed him and slipped inside the restaurant but not before she caught Cam trying not to laugh.

Yeah, well, he wasn't doing a whole lot better, she noticed as she stood in line to order. Sometimes Casper would run, but he'd stop often to sniff at something.

This was appalling behavior on the dog's part. Both Phyllis from the kennel and Kate had impressed on Zoey that she was the alpha and she must not lose her status. It seemed the Afghan breed could be real stinkers when

they wanted to be. Casper growling at her was totally unacceptable, although Zoey was afraid she'd lost her alpha
status as soon as Cam had rubbed his tummy. The thing
was, she completely understood because Cam sure had
alpha status with her.

Zoey ate part of her hamburger and watched Cam with
the dog. Casper's attitude was getting worse. Cam tried
to get something away from him without success. Zoey
didn't have to be a dog owner to realize that this behavior
had to stop. She shoved the rest of her hamburger into the
bag and pushed open the door.

Cam saw her coming. "Sorry." He held up a gray mass
before tossing it toward the Dumpster near where they'd
parked. "I think he ate a chicken nugget and part of the
box."

"Unauthorized food? Casper, you know better."

Casper stared down his nose at her.

"We're putting him in his crate," she said to Cam. "We
can't let him get away with this behavior."

"He's definitely been different today. He's already eaten
another chew toy and I had to pull over once and give him
food because I couldn't stand the licking sounds. Or the
whining."

Zoey blinked. "I slept through all that?"

Cam nodded.

"Did I snore?"

He shook his head.

"Liar."

He shook his head again. "Drooled a little."

"Eww." She grimaced as she yanked open the car door
and tossed in her food sack before shutting the door again.

"Kidding," Cam said.

"No, you aren't."

He laughed and she wasn't sure if she'd been right or

not. Stomping around to the rear of the SUV so her toes would regain some feeling, she decided she didn't want to know. "I'm getting the bitter-apple spray. His paws were looking raw, so I put some of the lemon-olive oil balm on them earlier and he must have liked the taste. Hey, don't let him do that!" Casper was trying to pull Cam back toward the Dumpster. "Tell him to heel."

"Casper, heel!" Cam bellowed. Casper resentfully glared at him before turning around and sitting on Cam's foot.

Zoey was pretty sure that wasn't the definition of "heel."

She unzipped her suitcase and took out the spray. "It'll probably take both of us to wrestle him into his crate. You take the front end and I'll take the back end."

She'd hoped Casper would respond to Cam better, but he didn't. She saw nothing resembling a potential Grand Champion in the bucking, yelping, wiggling animal. At one point, as they tried to get the squirming dog into the crate, Cam asked, "Why are we doing this again?"

"To demonstrate who's alpha."

"Yeah," Cam said. "I suspect he's figured out who's alpha."

That's what she was afraid of. Zoey used her shoulder to push a stiff-legged Casper into the crate. "He's a show dog. He shouldn't be acting like this."

Cam latched the door. "You must not be saying the magic words."

Casper peered through the screen at them, an expression of profound betrayal on his long-nosed doggy face.

"I don't think 'please' and 'thank you' would have worked," Zoey said as she hurried to the car and grabbed her jacket from the backseat.

A whump sounded as Cam closed the rear door and got in the driver's side. "A little late for that, isn't it?"

Zoey had draped the coat over her like a blanket. She shivered. "I know it's my turn to drive, but I'm too frozen!"

"Not a problem. You weren't supposed to wake up until Denver. Go back to sleep." He had to raise his voice as he said the last part because Casper was still whining about being in the crate.

Twenty miles later, Zoey was still awake and Casper was still whining—not as loudly, but much more pitifully.

Cam hadn't whined at all, and he was entitled. Any of her J boyfriends would have bailed long ago. What had she found attractive about them? Why had she been drawn to that type and not Cam's type? Was he so different on the outside?

Zoey studied him. He was a good-looking guy—better than good-looking, but in a more clean-cut way. Was that it? She subconsciously rejected the clean-cut guys because... She remembered their conversation about Cam being too saintly. She'd been kidding. Sorta. But had she believed the clean-cut types who had it together like her brother-in-law were too good for her?

Had she deliberately sought out losers who needed her help to avoid giving her all to Skin Garden? No, no, no. She wouldn't sabotage herself like that, would she? That was just messed up.

Or was she one of those girls who expected good guys to be boring and bad guys to be exciting? Cam hadn't been boring, certainly not last night. He hadn't looked as clean-cut that night in the airport, either. And that night he'd been... A little sound escaped her.

"What?" he asked.

"I kinda miss the scruffy beard. I realize it's not your style, and so many guys wear it now, it's lost its edge. But it suited you. Just saying. In case you ever...you know."

"In case I ever what?"

She should have stopped after telling him it had suited him. "Change your…style." *Shut up, Zoey.*

"Hmm." After a silence, he said, "Do you enjoy kissing guys with a couple of days' growth of beard?"

"Not really. I end up with these red… Oh."

He grinned, and that grin didn't need a scruffy beard to be appealing.

All right then. A warmth that had nothing to do with the car's heater spread through her. Cam had accumulated a whole lot of good-guy points and that grin told Zoey it was only a matter of time before he'd want to cash them in. She wondered when. And how.

She had a few ideas. Zoey threw off the coat because those ideas made her plenty warm. She may have even broken a sweat. All she could think about was when and how and that if the driving conditions were better, the when might be now and the how would involve her unbuckling her seat belt and his jeans.

Why not now? Ahead of them, there were no cars. There was nothing but a long expanse of tire-tracked snowy highway cutting through farmland. She turned around to check behind them—no one. Casper had settled down.

Cam didn't *have* to drive as fast as they were going now. He could drop his speed by twenty, thirty miles an hour. A sedate speed. No one would notice any unsedate activity going on inside their car.

Zoey squirmed in her seat.

"You all right?" he asked.

"Oooh, I'm a little…stiff." She massaged her neck and rolled her shoulders. "Too long in one position." She shifted until she faced him. "The scenery never changes, does it? This must be a boring drive for you."

"It's okay."

"It could be more than okay." She paused and lowered her voice. "A lot more than okay."

"Are you talking about car games?" he asked carefully.

"Yes." Zoey bunched her coat over the console between the seats. "Grown-up car games."

Cam glanced at the coat and then up at her. Their eyes held for a beat before he jerked his attention back to the road. "Does this game have any rules?"

"You have to keep your hands on the wheel."

Cam stilled. Zoey reached across the console and ran her fingers lightly over his thigh.

His knuckles went white. "Zoey."

And that's all he said. She couldn't tell from the way he said her name whether he meant, "Go for it" or "Are you crazy?" or "I'm stunned speechless by my good fortune" or "I'm not that kind of guy." Except she was pretty sure all guys were "that kind of guy."

Maybe he hadn't thought she was "that kind of girl." But, again, what guy wouldn't like "that kind of girl"?

"Cam?"

Without taking his eyes from the road, he lifted her palm to his face and kissed it.

Good answer.

Zoey trailed her fingers down his chest to his waistband and kept going. He flinched and the car jumped.

"I'm going to slow down," he said and eased up on the accelerator. "But you don't have to."

Smiling, Zoey tap danced her fingers over the bulge in his jeans. As she unsnapped the waistband, she said, "I spy with my little eye…something not so little."

With an unintelligible sound, Cam shifted to give her easier access. Zoey worked the zipper down and reached inside. At her touch, Cam's breath hissed between his teeth.

Zoey felt pure feminine satisfaction as she stroked the length of him and listened to his breathing come faster.

She unbuckled her seat belt. "I'm now officially a law-breaker," she murmured as it recoiled.

Scooting to the edge of the bucket seat, she reached across with her other arm to peel away layers of jeans, tucked-in shirt and undershorts while maintaining a steady, rhythmic stroking.

Not so easy. He was hard and smooth and so far away. Zoey was already uncomfortable from leaning forward with her arms extended, not that she should notice. But she did. Unbuckling her seat belt hadn't helped. She hadn't realized the logistics would present such a problem. The gear shift was right in the middle and the generous distance between the two bucket seats wasn't making things any easier. She felt herself slipping on the leather and gripped him harder. Damn SUV. "It's so big!"

"Thank you," he said in a hoarse voice.

"Well, I meant the car…" *Shut up, Zoey.* "But you're pretty impressive yourself." *Shut up, Zoey.* She leaned forward, squeezed past the gear shift, which was wedged against her ribs, and lowered her head. Her mouth landed on his thigh, regrettably short of her goal. She inched forward, but kept slipping back because of the leather seats.

"Ah—"

In horror, Zoey realized she'd been gripping him to anchor herself. She jerked her hands away. "I'm so sorry!"

"It's…okay," he said, sounding not okay.

She wiggled and braced herself. "I just can't…seem… to get there."

"I've heard that before," Cam muttered.

With renewed determination, Zoey heaved herself onto the console between the seats. And hit her head on the car roof. "Ow."

"Zoey…"

"I got this." She stuffed her coat against the door so she wouldn't slide back as far.

"I'm not sure I want you to have it," Cam said.

And, to be blunt, there wasn't that much to have anymore. "I can't believe this." Mortified, Zoey sat up in her seat. "I'm so sorry." What a mistake. Could there be a more awkward, humiliating *disaster* of a seduction?

Cam drew a deep breath. And then another. "It was a great idea. It was a fantastic idea…but the time had not yet come."

A beat went by. "I do not believe you just said that."

"I've been hanging around my cousin too much."

"Is this where I ask you how it's hanging?"

Cam made a garbled sound. It might have been laughter. It might have been a sob. It might have been both. "Rain check?"

"Absolutely. I'd say anytime, anyplace, but…" She trailed off as a fresh wave of embarrassment washed over her.

Once again, she'd tried to take advantage of an opportunity and in spite of her best intentions, it had turned out to be just another mistake. When would she learn that when she got an idea, she should do exactly the opposite?

"Let's go for another time in another place," Cam said, adjusting his jeans.

Zoey leaned her head against the seat and closed her eyes. "I am so embarrassed."

"Don't be. You know why?"

She shook her head.

"Because you just gave me the world's best rain check."

9

Zoey smiled weakly. He'd probably never cash that rain check in. "Why am I a failure at everything?"

"Am I going to have to give you the Babe Ruth speech?"

Zoey opened her eyes. "What's that?"

"Babe Ruth is famous for hitting seven hundred and fourteen home runs," Cam informed her. "It was a record for more than fifty years. Do you know how many times he struck out?"

She shook her head.

"One thousand three hundred and thirty. And that was also a record at the time. But only motivational speakers remember that statistic."

"I've got the strikeouts. I just don't have any home runs," Zoey mumbled.

"But what I admire about you is that you keep stepping up to the plate."

"Okay. No more baseball metaphors."

Cam laughed. "Gotcha."

He was being incredibly decent about the whole incident, but Zoey was still too mortified to make conversation.

In the silence, she heard someone's stomach making

noises, and at first she assumed it was hers because she was so upset. Then she was afraid the sounds were coming from Cam because of, um, stuff with nowhere to go. But soon she heard a roiling groan that was too loud to ignore. She opened her eyes and sat up to find Cam darting glances toward her.

Horrible, awful, disgusting sounds gurgled behind them.

"Casper," they said in unison.

"He's going to throw up!" Zoey pointed. "Pull over!"

Cam slowed. "There's not really a place…I can't make out the edge of the road…"

Casper made a series of hacking coughs.

"Just pull over anywhere!" she shouted as Cam drove to the shoulder and stopped. The car slid a little and came to rest at an angle.

Zoey threw open the door and plunged knee-deep into snow. Slipping and sliding, she tried to make her way to the back of the car. Cam beat her there. He already had the door open and was working at the latch on the crate.

"Wait. I have to get his leash—"

Casper pushed his way out and leaped from the car. Just his head poked above the snow and then only briefly as he bounded off, fortunately toward the field and not toward the highway.

"Casper!" they both shouted. Zoey took off after him but promptly fell to her knees and inhaled snow. Cam gripped the car bumper and shouted for Casper.

They heard hacking sounds. Zoey struggled to her feet and trudged toward the noises. Behind her Cam said, "I'll take care of the crate."

Zoey stopped and turned around. "I can*not* ask you to do that. Seriously."

Cam ignored her and dragged the crate out of the car.

And there, by the side of a road in the wilds of Nebraska, standing knee-deep in snow as she watched the object of her disastrous, failed seduction clean out a dog crate with a fast-food paper bag, Zoey had a revelation: she could love this guy. True, spend-the-rest-of-your-life-with love. The for-better-or-worse kind of love. The in-sickness-and-in-health love. And he must feel the same way because nothing said love like cleaning dog vomit out of a crate when it wasn't even your dog. No rain check was worth that.

For the first time in her life, Zoey was in a real, grown-up relationship. That was the difference between Cam and her J boyfriends. Maturity. In a grown-up relationship, it was easier to deal with all the bad, unpleasant things that came your way because you were together. And all the good things would be even better.

Tears came to her eyes, but she was going to pretend it was the wind.

"Casper. To me," she said. Didn't shout. Didn't plead. Spoke with a "firm expectation of being obeyed." She heard a crunchy rustling and hoped it was the sound a large, hairy dog makes when plowing through snow. Moments later something brushed against her. That something better be Casper.

She saw a black nose and a couple of blue elastic bands. "Poor guy." She reached down to pat his head and he licked her frozen hand. She tried not to dwell on what had recently passed over that tongue as they made their way to the car.

Cam was hoisting the crate back inside. "I did the best I could, but it'll need more cleaning before you get on the plane."

Something else Zoey didn't want to contemplate. "I'm

not sure he should be flying." She watched as the dog clambered up to the road's shoulder. "Oh, ick, Casper."

Using one of his dirty coats and snow, she attempted to clean his front legs. The mess would have been a whole lot worse if his coat had been loose, but it was bad enough. A horrible thought occurred to her. "I put lemon balm on his feet." She looked up at Cam. "My lemon balm poisoned him!"

Cam shook his head. "No, this one is on me. He got that chicken nugget box."

"A chicken nugget isn't going to cause—" She gestured. "Mt. Vesuvius. What if he's sick? I mean *sick* sick? Should we find a vet somewhere?" Before she caught herself, she scanned the empty, snowy landscape as though a veterinarian would magically appear.

Cam had walked off and reappeared with her coat. Draping it over her shoulders, he grabbed Casper's collar so Zoey's arms were free to shrug into the sleeves.

"He could have snarfed down something else I didn't notice," Cam said. "On the other hand I cleaned a lot of chew toy out of the crate."

Their eyes met. "Kate did say they were emergency only. How many has he eaten?"

"Three?"

Zoey sighed. "Stupid dog." She wadded up Casper's coat, wishing she could ditch it, and got the bitter apple spray out of the suitcase.

Casper whined.

"Yeah, you know what this is, don't you?" She eyed the crate. "Let's not force him in there. At this point, it doesn't much matter."

Cam stared into the formerly pristine interior of the rental. "Agreed."

"Up." She gestured and Casper jumped into the car

without struggling and curled onto his side. He didn't even protest when Zoey sprayed his paws.

Once inside the car, she got out her cell phone, relieved to find that she didn't have reception. Now she could avoid reporting to Kate.

"I've got a signal." Cam offered her his phone.

"I'm going to pretend I didn't hear that."

"Chicken." He started the car.

"Don't say that word."

"Oh, come on. I think we're unfairly maligning the food of one of the great institutions of our country."

He surprised a laugh out of her. "I can't believe you're making jokes when we're all wet and dirty and it stinks in here."

"We're also stuck. And that's no joke." Cam rocked the car back and forth, but the wheels couldn't get any traction.

"That explains the 'soft shoulder' signs." As far as relationships went, she and Cam had experienced plenty of "for worse." She was ready for some "for better."

"Here. You take over." Cam unbuckled his seat belt. "I'm going to get out and push."

"No." Zoey held up a hand to stop him. "My boots and jeans are already soaked. *I'll* get out and push."

Cam looked doubtful, which made Zoey all the more determined. She slammed the door and made her way around to the rear of the SUV. Her toes were numb, which might be a good thing if, say, the car rolled onto them.

Cam stuck his head out of the window. "Stand away. I'm going to rock the car. Wait to push until I give the signal."

"What's the signal?" she yelled over the engine.

"Push."

"Wait!" Zoey had noticed the slick, muddy ruts the tires had made. "Let me get some dried grass and gravel to put under the tires."

"Great idea." He gave her a thumbs up.

Zoey agreed it was a great idea, but getting her fingers to bend was hard. She couldn't remember the last time she'd been this cold. Cam started to get out to help, but she waved him back inside. One of them had to be able to drive, and he was that one.

"Ready," she called, hoping the bits of road debris and frozen clods of Nebraska prairie would be enough to get them unstuck. If she'd been by herself, what would she have done? She didn't even have a cell signal to call a tow truck. And if she did, who would she call? She'd be stranded here waiting until a good Samaritan came by and helped her. And, sadly, living in an urban area had made her wary of good Samaritans.

Except Cam. Sure, she'd had a few nervous moments over the way he'd looked at her when they'd first met, but now she understood that intense gaze meant he was completely focused. And now when he trained it on her, it was more exciting than unnerving.

Cam rocked the car back and forth, back again and yelled, "Push!"

Zoey caught the forward motion and pushed with everything she had, channeling all those westward pioneers who'd pushed their wagons out of muddy creek banks—until she lost her footing and fell flat. Scrambling to her knees, her life flashed before her until the car gave a hop and rolled out of the rut.

Heart pounding, Zoey had another realization, right there on her knees in the slushy mud in the middle of America's heartland: she would have made a lousy pioneer.

"Zoey? You okay?" Cam called to her.

Nodding, she got to her feet and stumbled to the car. Her fingers were too frozen to pull the handle, so Cam had to reach across the seat and open the door for her.

Once inside, she leaned her head back. Her hair hung in wet strands and her feet squished inside her boots. "There is no way we're getting on a plane today, is there?"

"Doesn't matter," said the ever-steady Cam. "We were spending the night in Denver or Seattle anyway. So now it's Denver."

Zoey inhaled and nearly gagged. "Newsflash. We're not making it to Denver today."

TWO MISERABLE HOURS LATER, they'd found a dog-friendly motel and Cam had rented connecting rooms—not because he didn't intend to cash in his rain check, but because Casper required his own bathroom.

After carrying in their luggage, Cam left Zoey with the unenviable chore of washing Casper while he found some place to get the car cleaned inside and out. It took longer than he'd anticipated because they were in a little town and a lot of outdoor car washes closed down for the winter in Nebraska.

Eventually, he ended up at a car dealership that had a small branch of the same rental agency where he'd rented the SUV in Des Moines. They washed the car, out of pity more than anything, and let Cam use a hose on Casper's crate.

Now the car was clean and he was cold. Bone-deep cold. And his jeans were damp. They chafed. Cam wasn't a fan of chafing.

He was hungry, too. The rooms had a kitchenette with a microwave, so he bought some sandwiches and a six pack of locally brewed beer. Always beneficial to check out the competition. He passed by a Chinese restaurant and was suddenly tired of bread-based food, so he stopped and bought takeout. He had no idea if Zoey liked Chinese food, but he knew the important stuff about her. He knew she was someone who always had his back. He smiled to himself. She might crash into it and knock him down, but she'd be there, and she'd help him stand on his feet again, too.

Zoey was rock-solid dependable—maybe not always effective, but she tried. Not everyone did. Or they gave up too fast.

Cam had dated some gorgeous arm candy and couldn't name one of those past girlfriends who would have insisted on pushing the car. Or would have dropped everything to help her sister. They would have whined more than Casper about the delays and the inconvenience they'd gone through. But not once had Zoey ever whined or ever considered giving up.

He could still hear her insisting that he go on without her in Des Moines, and briefly flashed to the very blonde, very stacked, very demanding Trisha he'd dated very briefly, and only because Gus had pushed him into it. He didn't have to try hard to imagine Trisha at the airport wailing, "Caaaam…you aren't going to leeeeeave me, are you?"

And then into the imaginary scene walked Zoey ordering Trisha to sit and stay.

The image made him laugh. Zoey wouldn't have put up with Trisha's whining for an instant. And Cam hadn't for much longer.

In spite of her so-called mistakes, Zoey was the one he wanted on his team. And by his side…or beneath him. Or on top of him. That little episode in the car had surprised the hell out of him. Excited the hell out of him, too. And even though nothing—and no one—had come from it, his frustration had melted at the sight of her obvious embarrassment. Yeah, those pink cheeks had roused all sorts of tender, protective feelings for her.

And he had a rain check to look forward to.

Cam no longer noticed that he was chafed, and he was no longer cold. And who cared about Chinese food when he had that kind of a rain check? He imagined stretching out on a nice comfortable bed, naked, with Zoey bent over him. Also naked. His heart sped up and his blood pulsed hotly as his damp jeans grew tight. In a minute they'd be steaming. He could practically feel Zoey's hair brushing over his thighs, his stomach…her hot mouth closing over his—

A car horn sounded and Cam realized he'd been sitting at a green light. He accelerated through the intersection but had no idea where he was or where their motel was located because he'd been fantasizing about rain checks instead of paying attention to where he was driving. It was a good thing the motel's address was on the plastic key tag so he could use the car's GPS to find his way back.

Cam carried the food and beer into his room and noticed that Zoey had opened the connecting door. He could hear running water from the bathroom and her murmuring to Casper.

"Hi, honey, I'm home," he sang and set the food next to the sink by the microwave.

"Casper!"

"Nope. It's Cam."

A body—no doubt a wet dog—thumped against the bathroom door.

"Casper! Get back in the tub!"

Cam winced. "When you're ready, come on through. I've got Chinese food." Which Casper had no doubt smelled.

"I *love* Chinese food!" he heard.

Cam smiled to himself. They could play the fortune-cookie game. In bed.

In the meantime, he intended to hit the shower.

He was toweling off when he heard Zoey call, "Can you bring the hairdryer from your bathroom?"

He slicked back his hair, pulled on a pair of jeans, even though she'd already seen the important stuff, and unplugged the hairdryer from the wall unit.

Padding through to the other room, he knocked on the bathroom door. "Hairdryer delivery."

Casper barked.

"Stay, Casper." Zoey's voice was right at the door. It opened about an inch. "Can you help me? With both of us drying, it'll go a lot faster. This dog has seriously thick hair."

"Sure. Let me—" Put on a T-shirt was what he'd been going to say, but Casper nosed open the door and escaped, brushing past Cam on the way out.

"Casper, no! Grab him—he's wet!"

Cam grabbed for the dog with the hand that wasn't holding the hair dryer, but Casper slipped out of his grasp.

"Darn it, Casper!" Zoey stumbled as she ran out of the bathroom. Casper shook violently and Zoey turned away, holding out her hands to shield herself.

Her hands were no match for the spray, but then again she was already pretty wet.

"Casper…" She wiped her hands on her top and brushed at her arms.

Cam's mouth went dry. If he weren't so focused on Zoey, he would have appreciated the irony. She'd prepared for Casper's bath by bunching her hair into a sloppy ponytail and stripping down to her underwear, which consisted of turquoise-blue panties and a tight white tank top heavily splotched with water. The splotches revealed that there was nothing else beneath the tank but Zoey.

"Casper!"

Snorting, the dog shook his head and rubbed his nose and face along the carpet.

"Come here!" Zoey slapped her thigh. She had miles of legs that disappeared into a cute little tush.

"Don't make me drag you back in there." When Casper ignored her, she stalked over to him and bent down, prepared to make good on her threat.

Cam tried to swallow and couldn't. Those turquoise bikini panties were completely transparent, and the front of the tank mostly so. It had ridden up to expose a crescent of bare skin at her lower back. As he watched, the crescent widened and Cam's fingertips tingled at the thought of helping it along.

Zoey wrestled with Casper, who barked and treated the whole thing like a game. The dog got away from her and galloped through the connecting door, Zoey running after him. Cam heard them race around the room and then Casper was headed through the door again, zooming straight toward him. Casper stopped, barked and took off just as Zoey reappeared.

"I could use a little help here."

Cam froze.

She was breathing hard, and her top clung damply and transparently. He should point that out, but she was so sexy, she stole his breath, along with the ability to speak or move.

She could make a living entering wet T-shirt contests. She could make a *fortune* entering wet T-shirt contests.

Casper ran in and out of the room again before positioning himself exactly between the two rooms and wildly contorting as he rubbed his back on the carpet.

"Casper!" she said in exasperation. "Help me get him into the bathroom, Cam?"

Cam grinned. "Later."

"Why?"

He stepped to the side so Zoey could see herself in the mirror.

She squeaked and crossed her arms over her chest. "Why didn't you say something?"

Cam set the hairdryer on the lamp desk. "Because I figured you'd do that." He walked toward her.

She retreated. "Cam...there's a wet dog running around."

"By now he's only a damp dog."

"I don't want him to be cold and uncomfortable."

"Are you cold and uncomfortable?"

She rubbed her arms. "Well, yeah, kind of."

"I can fix that." Cam cupped her face and kissed her, inching forward until her wet chest pressed against his. Her lips were cold and he kissed her until they warmed and parted. He slipped his tongue inside her mouth and stroked hers.

She shuddered and pulled away. "We should really dry him off." Her voice lacked conviction.

Cam moved his hands to her upper arms and rubbed until the goose bumps disappeared. "He'll dry on his own."

Zoey made a little noise and dropped her head back. Cam nuzzled her neck. "But his coat will be all crinkled."

"It'll get crinkled in the ponytail holders anyway." He nipped at the sensitive place just beneath her ear.

She sucked a breath between her teeth. "Cam, Casper is my responsibility. You said you understood."

And he'd never regretted a promise more than he did at this moment.

They heard scratching sounds and looked through the connecting door to see Casper pawing at the pillows on the bed in Cam's room before turning around a couple of times and collapsing. He gave a great sigh and was still.

"He seems very comfortable on that bed," Cam said, and felt Zoey relax in his arms.

"Yes." She smiled and his blood heated. "Isn't it great that we've got a spare?"

She popped the button on his jeans and eased down the zipper. "You dressed quickly."

"Not as fast as I can undress." Cam shoved at his jeans and kicked them off. Then he ran his fingers along Zoey's ribcage and kissed her until she sighed and raised her arms.

Cam pulled off the tank and tossed it over his shoulder. Gazing at her, he said, "You're so beautiful, I can't think."

"Did you think to bring a condom?"

He nodded.

Zoey freed her hair and shook it over her shoulders. "Get it."

10

CAM RETURNED QUICKLY, in time to help Zoey pull down the comforter. She straightened and started to wiggle out of her panties.

"Wait."

She raised her eyebrows and he grinned. "Leave 'em on."

"They're still damp."

"It doesn't matter. I'm kind of digging the turquoise."

Zoey glanced down at herself and then moved her hand under the waistband. "Oh, you are, are you?"

"Yeah." He loved the way her underwear was supposed to conceal but didn't hide a thing.

Cam held out his arms and she walked into them. "You're beautiful, Zoey." He threaded strands of her hair between his fingers. "You know the difference between pretty and beautiful?"

"Tell me."

"Beauty is deeper and richer. More complex and longer lasting. Pretty makes you happy. You enjoy pretty as long as it's around. Then you forget about it until you find the next pretty thing. But beauty haunts you. It's compelling and unforgettable. It gets under your skin and in your head and draws you to it. Pretty fades. Beauty ripens. With it, your life is richer. Without it, you're existing, not living. You need it. You want it. And when you find it, you hold on." He looked deep into her eyes so she could see he meant what he said. "You're the most beautiful woman I've ever met, Zoey."

"Cam…" She blinked rapidly and fanned her eyes. "That was…no one has ever…" She sniffed. "Wow."

She fanned at her eyes again and gave him a wobbly smile. "You," she began, sticking her finger in the middle of his chest, "are a master seducer." She pushed until he fell onto the bed, taking her with him.

She kissed her way down his stomach. "Your beauty speech was inspirational." She rolled him onto his back and straddled him. "And I am inspired."

He cupped her face and held her still. "I meant every word."

She grasped his wrists, pulled his hands away from her face and pinned them above his head. "That's what's so inspirational."

He gazed up at her breasts. "The view from here is inspirational, too." He tried to lever himself within kissing distance and managed to swipe a nipple with his tongue before she stretched out of reach.

"No, no," she said. "You've been taking care of me for days, so now I'm going to take care of you."

Cam was no longer flexible. And because Zoey and her turquoise bikini panties were sitting on his most inflexible part, she knew it, too. "That's right." She rubbed against him and spoke in a sultry voice. "This is all about you."

"What about your breasts?" Cam asked, eyeing them. "Can they be about me, too?"

She drew closer but stayed out of touching range.

He tugged his arm experimentally, but she held his wrist

in place. "Relax. I'm in charge. You don't have to do anything but feel." She shimmied her shoulders suggestively and lowered herself until she brushed her chest against his.

Cam was both hot and cold at the same time. Or maybe he was so hot it felt like cold. He pulsed his groin against her turquoise warmth but she lifted herself away. Now the only parts of her body touching him were her hands on his wrists.

Unacceptable.

He licked his lips, dry because he'd been practically panting. "Is this one of those you've-been-a-bad-boy things?"

"No." Zoey shook her head. "Because you've been a very good boy." Her hair rippled over her shoulders and got in the way of Cam's view of her breasts.

She had great breasts. He tried to remember what they'd felt like that night in the terminal; the memory seemed to be the only thing he was going to get for a while. He blew her hair out of the way, exposing her nipples again, and he was gratified when they tightened. Glad to know he had *some* effect on her.

"Oh," she said softly.

He was pretty sure it was a good "oh."

"You're very resourceful."

He was very desperate. He understood why she wanted to take the lead, but he'd been holding himself back since she'd unzipped his pants in the car.

Zoey bent over him, her hair falling around him exactly the way he'd fantasized. Since running his hands over her bare skin had also been part of the fantasy, he reached for her, forgetting that she'd pinned his arms over his head.

"Uh-uh." To keep his arms down, she had to lean forward, which happily brought her breasts within a tongue's length of his mouth.

He swiped at one hard tip and heard her inhale sharply, so he did it again. And again.

"Mmm." It was a purr and she stretched like a cat before lowering herself to give him free access at last.

Cam drew as much of her into his mouth as he could, entirely focused on using his tongue to drive her mindless with pleasure so she'd let go of his arms and they could both become mindless with pleasure. Because so far, Cam had only been mindless with anticipation and need. He *needed* to touch her. He *needed* to see her wild for him. He *needed* to bury himself within her and feel her throbbing around him.

And he needed release.

With a groan, she pulled away, her cheeks flushed and her eyelids heavy. "You're very distracting."

"I can be a lot more than distracting."

"Oh, I'm sure." She bit her bottom lip and sat up.

One breast was rosy and wet from his mouth and the other looked sadly neglected. "Come here."

She shook her head, hair rippling.

"Ah, Zoey."

She inched backward as far as she could before lowering her head and kissing his throat, continuing to kiss a slow trail down his chest—too slow for Cam. His muscles clenched and he brought his knees up, intending to capture her between them, but Zoey stopped. "No touching," she warned.

Slowly, Cam let his legs fall and Zoey gave him another of her maddeningly slow kisses, watching him as she did so. The lower she went, the more of her turquoise-covered rear popped up behind her. She paused, watching him watch her, and wiggled it suggestively.

He was going to explode like some teenager.

"I have a problem," she said and Cam's heart stopped.

"This is as far as I can reach and still hold your wrists."

"Then let them go."

She sat up. "Still no touching. Promise?"

"No! I appreciate the games, but you're killing me! Enough."

She shook her head. "Not until you promise."

"Zoey!" He reached for her but dropped his arm as she levered herself off him. He fully expected her to climb out of the bed.

"Zoey, I'm—" His breath hissed between his teeth as she took him into her mouth. He hadn't been expecting that, at least not right then.

She caressed him and swirled her tongue around him as though he were a human ice-cream cone. No ice-cream cone could keep from melting under that tongue, and neither could he.

"Ahh, Zoey." He dropped his head back onto the pillow and abandoned himself to the sensations.

She tightened and loosened her grip and varied the rhythm of her tongue and lips, heating him up and cooling him off until her tongue flicked lightly on a spot that almost had him levitating off the bed. As it was, he fisted his hands in the sheets and gasped. He felt a tremor and knew he was close. Forcing his eyes open, he locked on hers. "I want the first time to be inside you." As she nodded and slipped off the turquoise panties, he grabbed for the condom but Zoey gracefully retrieved it and ripped it open, clearly not trusting his shaking fingers.

Smart thinking on her part.

"I'm not usually so…" He gestured vaguely as she sheathed him.

"It's a heck of a compliment and a pretty effective turn-on." She straddled him. "Oh—we're finished with the no-touching part."

Immediately, Cam's hands latched onto her hips and eased her down. Slowly her warmth surrounded him until he was all the way inside her body. They stilled, looking into each other's eyes. Keeping his gaze locked on hers, Cam began a slow, rhythmic pulsing, watching as her eyes went a little glassy. She may believe this was all about him, but he wanted to give her pleasure, too. With unexpected insight, he realized his own enjoyment depended on it.

Increasing the pace, he thrust up to meet her downward strokes. Zoey's hands covered his where he gripped her hips. He loosened his fingers in case they were digging into her too much, but she pressed against them and shifted slightly.

"Oh!" Her eyes widened and she paused before tentatively moving again. "Ohh." She smiled a dreamy smile and moved faster.

That dreamy smile made Cam sweat. He lifted her higher and brought her down harder as he drove into her.

"Oh, yes. That's the spot."

So he did it again. Harder.

"Mmm." She closed her eyes.

Her thigh muscles bunched and her breasts bounced as she took over the rhythm.

Her breasts. He was free to touch them now. Cam slid his hands from beneath hers and covered them.

The breath hissed between Zoey's teeth as she arched, pressing into his palms. Her nipples were hard and when he rubbed them, she moaned and dropped her head back.

Cam's pulse pounded in his ears and he had to slow down to keep from going over the edge. Moments ago, he'd wanted things to move faster; now he wanted to savor these moments with Zoey naked on top of him, fiercely concentrating on her own pleasure. Every moan, every time she bit her lip, every panting breath fueled his passion, too. He wanted to see her climb higher and higher until she peaked. He wanted to watch her face as she was suspended in that everlasting instant before pleasure rippled through her.

Sweat slicked their bodies and their breaths came in short gasps. Just before his control slipped away, Cam clutched Zoey's hips and ground her against him as he gave two quick hard thrusts.

"Cam!" Her eyes opened in surprise. "Oh! Ohh…" They drifted shut again as her muscles clenched around him.

He held himself still until the pulses faded away and she opened her eyes once more. Smiling she rocked against him, and with another thrust, he exploded. The intensity caught him by surprise, although it shouldn't have. He rode wave after pounding wave until he could breathe again. Until he could speak again. And when he could, all he said was, "Zoey," and hoped it was enough.

"I know." She climbed off and curled up next to him. "Epic, huh?"

He draped an arm around her. "Beyond epic."

"That sounds like a good name for a sequel."

There was going to be a sequel. Cam smiled.

They dozed but not for long before a sound woke Cam.

"Did you hear something?" Zoey asked beside him.

"Paper?"

They listened, and then Cam suddenly remembered. "The Chinese food!" He bolted from the bed, Zoey right behind him.

They found Casper attacking one of the bags. He'd pulled it off the counter and onto the floor. It was the *last* of the bags he'd pulled off the counter and onto the floor.

"Casper!" Zoey squealed and dashed over to him.

Guilt and a sick feeling in the pit of his stomach kept Cam from appreciating the fact that Zoey was naked. She was going to blame herself for becoming distracted. And blame Cam for distracting her.

Casper ducked his head and didn't resist when Zoey snatched the bag and plastic dish away from him. He was probably full anyway. Cam started picking up the remains of the food. Casper had even chewed on the packets of soy sauce, which accounted for the dark brown splotches on the carpet.

"I'm going to have to call Kate," Zoey told him with a worried glance at the dog.

"I'm sorry," Cam said. "I didn't think he could reach stuff on the counter."

"I didn't, either."

They surveyed the kitchenette, where one of the two plastic chairs had been pulled or, more likely, nosed away from the table just enough for a large dog to hop from it to the table on his way to the counter. Cam almost admired Casper's cleverness. Almost.

"I'll clean off his face and then call my sister." Zoey's shoulders slumped.

"Do not—" Cam took her by the shoulders and turned her to face him. "Do *not* blame yourself for sleeping with me." If she did, there'd never be an epic sequel.

She smiled. "Okay."

"Good." But he wasn't entirely convinced. "I didn't get any dishes that would have had bones, and most of the packaging is still intact. Mangled, but intact." He tilted up her chin. "And there are sandwiches in the fridge."

"Thanks." She dropped a quick kiss on his knuckles before scolding Casper for licking at the carpet.

"I'll clean that up while you deal with him." And then Cam was treated to the view of Zoey's backside as she walked away from him. He watched her usher the dog through the connecting door. Just before she walked through herself, she looked over her shoulder, gave him a smoldering stare and wiggled her butt.

Cam drew in a deep breath. He was so ready for Beyond Epic.

11

RARELY DID A sequel surpass the original, but Beyond Epic was truly *beyond epic*.

Cam had been determined that Zoey wouldn't blame herself for having sex when she should have been watching Casper. Of course, she still blamed herself, but she didn't regret it. Cam had been so passionately giving and tender… Remembering it now, while walking Casper around the motel parking lot, tears came to her eyes. He'd made love to her—all of her, but especially her heart. All this time, Zoey had been having sex. Oh, she'd thought she'd been making love. On her part it had been love, or what she assumed was love, but maybe it had just been hope. Now she understood the difference. Over the years, she'd settled because she didn't know there could be more. If it weren't for Cam, she might *never* have known. She tried to explain to him how she felt, but she only got all emotional. He didn't seem upset. He'd just given her a meltingly gentle look, gathered her in his arms and let her blubber all over his chest.

Maybe he was used to having women get all emotional. Because, maybe, he was just that good.

Immediately, Zoey was struck by an almost insane

amount of jealousy at the idea of Cam making any other woman as happy and sated as he'd made her. And she sure didn't want to feel that way with any other man. She gave a harsh laugh that sent a white cloud into the cold Nebraska morning. As if she would *ever* feel that way with anyone but Cam.

She knew him better than she'd known any other man, even the J boyfriend she'd lived with. The Js hadn't truly known her, either, she admitted. She'd held back part of herself, waiting to experience the deep, emotional connection they'd need to build a life together.

Well, that hadn't happened. And she'd wasted a whole lot of years trying to make it happen.

"How are you doing, Casper?" She idly scratched his head. "Up to a jog?"

Zoey took off, the cold air filling her lungs and clearing her head.

Cam was different. But she could end up exactly the same way—abandoning Skin Garden in order to make a relationship work. He had a busy life. Too busy.

Case in point: his cousin Gus had called this morning in a panic about the regular Saturday brewery tour and beer tasting.

Cam had the phone on speaker while he'd done crunches on the floor—and hadn't that been a lovely breakfast treat—so Zoey had overheard their conversation as she got Casper ready to go outside. And she'd been a little shocked at hearing everything Cam was usually responsible for.

Over and over Gus had asked a variation of, "And who's to be doing that, I'd like to know?"

And over and over Cam had answered, "I usually do it, but since I'm not there, you'll have to."

"I can't do everything by myself! Who'll greet the customers and conduct the tour?"

"Plenty of MacNeils show up on Saturdays to help. It'll all work out, Gus."

Cam had been grinning—and sweaty—when he ended the call.

Zoey had paused on her way out the door. "You enjoyed that."

"I did."

"But, Cam, you're not an it'll-all-work-out kind of person."

"I am not. Gus is, though. And I have been dying to say that to him. It should be an interesting Saturday." He stretched his arms over his head and sprawled in the desk chair.

"Based on my extensive experience, I'd say it'll be a disaster."

"I'm counting on it." He opened his laptop.

"Why, Mr. MacNeil, you do have a devious streak."

Looking devious, he reached for her and Zoey danced out of the way because she knew where *that* would lead and Casper had already given her the stink eye for letting him stand by the door this long.

"I will say that this is the first time someone has *hoped* for a disaster," she said.

"Everything will be okay once they open the taps, but it should make my point," Cam said. "I'm not discounting Gus's contribution. He's a fantastic salesman, which is why I want him on my side when I insist that we hire an office manager. Experiencing the horror of extended manual labor should make him very convinced."

He leaned back in the chair as the laptop booted up. "Joyce was right. I haven't been following my own business plan. It's past the point for the brewery to have a paid, full-time office manager instead of relatives coming in for a few hours whenever they have the chance. But that takes cash, and it's got to come from somewhere." He tilted his head. "Know anyone who'd want a job as an office manager in a small, up-and-coming brewery?"

By the way he smiled at her, Zoey understood what he was suggesting. And she wanted to agree with him. She wanted to throw her arms around his neck and say, "I do! Then we could be together all day long and wouldn't that be perfect?" or some such garbage. Only she didn't because it wouldn't.

It would be a mistake. A huge mistake.

Casper had whined then, thank goodness, so she'd escaped with a cheery, "No, but I'll keep my ears open," which she hoped hadn't sounded as fake to Cam as it had to her.

She felt the familiar pull to entwine herself in his life, to give up both her call-center job and her creams and lotions. It was her usual pattern as she sought that elusive connection, the one on which she and her guy could build a life.

With Cam, she already had that deep, emotional connection. In fact, they'd connected so quickly on so many levels, it was difficult to process. Their relationship was on fast forward because they'd spent days in each others' company under conditions that revealed a person's true nature. She liked Cam's true nature. A lot.

They were even being practical, at least during the blissful moments of sated lust, discussing how they should see each other in their regular lives so they could test if what they felt was real and lasting. But they both were already sure it was.

The question was, what were they going to do about it?

The answer wasn't as simple as Cam probably assumed—picking up where they left off once they both returned to Texas. Even though she had a long way to go, Zoey still wanted to achieve a modest success on her own before she merged her life with someone else's. If she abandoned Skin Garden yet again to work with Cam, then when MacNeil's really took off, it would be his success. Not hers.

Zoey stopped jogging when she sensed Casper slowing. She walked him to the grassy edge of the parking lot, where he squatted and noxious fumes filled the air.

Chinese food did not agree with Casper, and that was an understatement.

When he was finished, Zoey took a picture with her cell phone, as instructed, and sent it to Kate and Ryan. Moments later, her phone played "Who Let the Dogs Out," which made her laugh. Cam had programmed it as her sister's ring tone. "Hi, Kate."

"Zoey, do you think you could zoom in a little?"

Zoey closed her eyes. "Kate, I am not going to send you close-ups of your dog's poop."

"Well, I'm *sorry* if you find it unpleasant, but if you'd been watching him the way you should have, you wouldn't have to be taking pictures of dog poop." Self-righteous and nasty. Vintage Kate.

"Or maybe I shouldn't have called you in the first place."

"There shouldn't have been anything to call me about! But I knew there would be. I just knew this was a mistake."

The familiar yoke of guilt settled around her, but Zoey threw it off. "Then *why* did you ask me?" Her voice was shrill in the morning silence. Probably everyone in the motel could hear her, including Cam.

"Because I figured even *you* could manage to do something this simple! Everything was all planned. And where are you? Nebraska. I do not see Nebraska on the itinerary!"

Zoey took a deep breath and let it out. "Because I thought—"

"I told you not to think!"

The familiar sense of defeat flooded her. Why had she believed this time would be different? A knot, equal parts guilt and the awful motel-room coffee, formed in her stomach. She was going to be sick. How convenient that Casper had paved the way. "I'm sorry," she whispered.

"Zoey." It was Ryan.

"I'm sorry." She apologized to him, too.

"Are you kidding? Nobody else would have done this for us."

"I know. That's why I'm apologizing."

"You have nothing to apologize for. But your sister does. Don't hang up."

Oh, great. As though a forced apology from Kate would make her feel any better.

"Zoey? I'm so sorry."

Was that tiny little voice *Kate's?*

"I didn't mean any of those things."

Zoey exhaled. "You meant them. You just didn't mean to say them out loud."

"No, I—it's the hormones. They're making me crazy. You should hear some of the awful stuff I've said to Ryan!"

"No, she shouldn't," Ryan said in the background.

"He's been so sweet," Kate cooed.

Zoey rolled her eyes.

"Tell her why," she heard him say and Zoey smiled. Sweet, but not a pushover. Like Cam, in a—

"Zoey, I'm pregnant!"

At first, Zoey thought she was talking about one of their dogs and tried to remember a female's name. Kate got all pissy when Zoey couldn't remember their dogs' names. And then the words sunk in. "You mean with a human baby?"

"No, a puppy," Kate said as Ryan roared with laughter in the background. "Yes, a baby!"

"Oh, Kate! When?"

They talked excitedly for a few moments. "So that's why I may have sounded more hyper than normal," Kate said.

"You sounded just the same to me." Zoey would let her get away with the hormone excuse for some of it, but not all. There had been plenty of other conversations when Kate hadn't been pregnant and had raged at Zoey.

Kate laughed but quickly noticed Zoey wasn't laughing with her. "Oh, come on, Zoey! I'll admit I've been a little snappish during our last few conversations, but now you understand why."

"What about all of our other conversations?"

Silence. At least Kate didn't deny it.

Zoey broke the silence. "I understand why you get angry and frustrated with me, but you should get rid of most of it before you spew it all over me."

"Zoey." Kate sounded hurt.

"You're a lot more than snappish, Kate," she said quietly.

There was another silence and Zoey suspected Kate had turned to Ryan. And from the soft gasp she heard next, her sister had found gentle confirmation in his face. He was that kind of man. Instinctively, she knew Cam was that kind of man, too.

"I'm sorry, Zoey. I'll try to be better. It's just there's so much happening—so much riding on this. It's still so unbelievable that Martha chose Casper for Alexandra's first litter. It would be an honor for him to breed with any of the Merriweather bitches, but Alexandra? It'll make Ryka's reputation. And Casper's, assuming all goes well. It's such a great opportunity, especially with the baby coming. And next week's show is major. Without Alexandra there, he's sure to win Grand Championship points!"

The potential Grand Champion was squatting again. Zoey decided not to inform Kate.

"There won't be as many opportunities to go to shows once the baby gets here." Kate was getting wound up again.

Ryan recognized the signals, too. Zoey could hear him murmuring.

"So tell me," she interrupted her sister. "What's the deal with the breeding thing? Do I have to do anything?" Oh, Lord, she hoped not. "Is there a special command?"

That last made Kate laugh. And then she proceeded to give Zoey more details than she ever wanted to know about breeding Afghan hounds.

The call came while Cam was checking the temperature at the Denver airport. He smiled, assuming it was Zoey, since she'd been outside for so long. He pressed the phone close because what he was going to say should be murmured in her ear, not surrounded by the tinny halo of the speaker setting. Fortunately, Richard's number registered in time for a last-second adjustment.

"Cameron MacNeil." He hoped the other man couldn't hear the surprise in his voice.

"Richard Campbell here," Richard said. "Are you in Seattle yet?"

Cam was caught off guard. "No. Nebraska."

"What are you doing in Nebraska?"

It was fortunate they weren't video conferencing. "Business. I rearranged my schedule." It was also fortunate that Zoey wasn't in the room. Cam could imagine her saying, "Liar, liar, pants on fire."

He grinned. She set his pants on fire, all right.

"Can you rearrange your schedule again to meet me at the hops farm?"

Cam's jaw clenched as a spurt of adrenaline shot

through him. *Richard was still interested.* And interested enough to leave Seattle for a field trip. The development was both unexpected and encouraging. Which also made it suspicious. But Richard's cash would enable Cam to reclaim part of his life and spend that part with Zoey.

He had to play his hand very carefully because the stakes were now much higher. *Keep it light but not too light,* he told himself. "I don't have to rearrange anything," he said to Richard. "I'm headed for the farm next."

"So you'll be keeping *that* appointment."

"And ours, too," Cam said.

"Please do." Richard went into his great-man-talking-to-lesser-mortals mode. "I don't often give second chances, but I happen to believe that friendship should count for something." .

"Absolutely."

They'd never been friends and Richard knew it. Cam wasn't about to fall into the trap of pretending they were. This was purely business, and if Richard didn't believe he'd receive value for his money, he wouldn't give Cam a cent or a second chance, friend or not.

However, Cam could be *friendly.* "How about we get some lunch afterward?"

"Sorry. I'm leaving for Seattle at noon. I have to catch a flight to London."

Of course he was. "I'll see you Friday then."

Cam had just raised his hand for a celebratory fist pump when Zoey burst through the other room's door.

"Cam!" She and Casper came bounding through the connecting door. "I talked with Kate.... What happened?" She'd caught him with his arms in the air.

"Richard rescheduled for Friday morning at the hops farm."

She looked confused. "And that's good?"

Yes, considering Cam hadn't expected him to reschedule at all. Zoey didn't know that, though. "It's unexpected."

"He must be really interested or he wouldn't go to the trouble." She knelt and unfastened Casper's coat.

"That's what I'm hoping, and that's what most people would assume. But this is Richard. He's well aware appearing eager will weaken his negotiating position."

"Why?"

"In business, the one who cares the most is willing to concede more to keep the other party from walking away," Cam said. "When you don't care, when you're willing to walk and the other side knows it, that's when you're strongest."

Zoey pulled off the coat and Casper headed for his water dish. "That's true in relationships, too. When you don't care anymore, when you're actually walking out the door with your stuff, *that's* when he promises to pick up his clothes and stop leaving dirty dishes all over the apartment."

Cam laughed. "Says the voice of experience?"

"Actually, no." Zoey gave him a wry smile as she stood. "He didn't promise anything. He said, 'Zoey don't be like this.' And I said, 'I'm not. That's why I'm leaving.' And he said, 'Fine. Whatever.' So I walked."

And he was very glad she had. "That's the thing. Sometimes, you gotta walk."

She gave him the strangest look. That was twice today and Cam wondered if he was missing something.

"What if it's a bad deal for the other party?" she asked. "Should you walk then?"

"Why?" He gave a short laugh. "That would be stupid."

"Not if you care more for the person involved than the deal."

They weren't talking about business deals anymore,

Cam realized. "It's up to the other party to decide whether a deal is bad."

"Yeah, well, the other party might—"

"Zoey." Cam stood, took Casper's silly coat out of her hands and tossed it onto the bed. Then he drew her to him. "Zoey," he said again and waited until she met his eyes. "What's this about?"

"You don't have to go to Seattle anymore."

It took him a moment. "I'd always planned to rent a car and drive from Seattle. Nothing has changed."

"Are you sure? I don't want to mess things up for you, Cam." She was serious. He could see the worry in her eyes, those huge green eyes. The ones he wanted to dive into.

He could kiss away the worry. They had time. The weather still had to warm up before Casper could fly anyway. Kissing away her worry was an *excellent* idea. He lowered his mouth and she heaved a great sigh.

"Cam, I'm serious."

He kissed an eyelid. "So am I."

"Cam." She pushed against his chest and, reluctantly, he let his arms fall away.

"I am a bad deal for you," she said earnestly. "I come with a long streak of failures."

"So break the streak."

"That's what I'm trying to do!"

"And I want to help you."

"You are. You have. But Cam, as much as I want to get this dog to Merriweather, it can't be at the expense of your meeting."

"It won't be." He reached for her again, but she swatted his hands away.

The anger in her expression burned through the lust haze.

"Listen to me," she said slowly and crisply. "This is a

chance for me to prove to myself and everyone else that I can succeed at something. I've told you that. But if you fail because you stay with me, it doesn't count."

"I understand," Cam said. And he did. He just didn't agree. If he failed, it was because he'd made the choice to fail. It wasn't her call. But he wasn't going to argue the point.

"You'd better," she said. "Because I want you to promise me that if we get to Denver and find out that we can't get on the same flight, you'll go on without me."

"If it makes a difference, sure."

She eyed him suspiciously. "What do you mean?"

"We've missed the morning flights. There's one at two-thirty, and since I have to turn in the car, that would be cutting it close. The next available flights all leave between four and seven. Whether I land in Seattle at seven o'clock or ten o'clock tonight doesn't make a difference."

"Promise me anyway."

"Zoey, be reasonable." As soon as he said the words, Cam knew they were a mistake.

Her jaw set. "Promise me, or I'll walk."

Cam grinned to himself. "I had a feeling you were going to say that." She'd rent another car and drive herself just to make a point. "Fine. I promise."

"Okay." She relaxed her shoulders a little. "And don't wait for me at the airport, either. I'm not staying in Seattle. I don't care how late it is, I'm driving to Ellensburg tonight. In fact, I'm driving all the way to Merriweather's front gate and sleeping the rest of the night in the car if I have to."

"You said Ellensburg? I noticed that name." Cam went to his laptop and brought up the state of Washington map. "Look. I'm headed to Mabton."

He pointed when Zoey came to stand next to him. "They're not that far apart." He typed in the cities and got driving directions between them. "An hour and a half drive, max."

Zoey stared at the map and then at him. She narrowed her eyes. "So?"

"So Richard has to leave by noon." He gestured to the screen. "The kennel is practically on the way back to Seattle."

"I'll be busy."

"I thought Casper was the one who's going to be busy. What is there for you to do?"

She gave him a tight smile. "Oh, I'm so glad you asked."

By the time they'd packed and loaded the car, Cam was regarding Casper with equal parts sympathy and awe.

"I bow to your courage," he said to Zoey as he pulled the SUV onto the highway again.

"Yeah," she said. "Notice Kate didn't mention all the details until now."

"A lot is at stake for them and they didn't want to put extra pressure on you. You'd have been tense and anxious, and dogs pick up on those emotions."

From behind them, snores sounded as Casper slept. "He's calm now because you're all loose and relaxed." Cam grinned. "I like to think I had something to do with that."

"A little something." Zoey stretched and yawned. "This morning has been an emotional rollercoaster. I need a nap already."

"Go for it."

"You don't mind?" She closed her eyes before she finished speaking and her breathing slowed almost immediately.

Which is how she missed Cam driving right past the cutoff to Denver.

12

Zoey got back into the car and slammed the door. Staring straight ahead, she said, "Smirk all you want to, but what you did was still wrong."

Cam hadn't realized he was smirking. Instead of starting the car, he faced her. If only he hadn't had to pull over for Casper, she would have still been asleep and they could have had this discussion when they were further down the road. As it was, they'd just passed Cheyenne, Wyoming, which was straight north of Denver, and it was only noon because of the time-zone change. They could reverse course on I25 and be at the airport in an hour and a half. Cam didn't want to point that out, however.

"Would you rather Casper had that little episode while in his crate at the airport? They probably wouldn't have let him on a plane."

Slowly, Zoey turned to glare at him. "That's not the point," she said. "You promised. *That's* the point."

"Technically, I promised if we got to Denver and I could take an earlier flight, I would."

Zoey took a breath before replying. "So because we're not in Denver you win on a technicality? Am I going to have to start looking for loopholes in your promises?"

"No!" She was so much angrier than Cam had expected her to be. "Forget I said that. I'm not trying to win. This," and he gestured to the road stretching endlessly in front of them, "seemed to be a better option at the time."

"Driving a thousand miles across a vast frozen wasteland in January seemed like a *better* option?"

"Yes." She might not believe him, but he had thoroughly analyzed driving versus flying. "The roads are clear, the sun is out, the forecast is good, and when you factor in the three-hour drive to Denver and the fact that we'd have to wait around to find out if we could get on a plane—"

"That's another thing—why didn't you book online when we were at the motel? Because of Casper, I couldn't, but *you* could have."

He'd hoped that wouldn't occur to her. "I wanted to have the option of getting on your flight *if it worked out,*" he stressed when she started to interrupt. "Besides, something could have gone wrong—"

"Such as not showing up at the airport?" she snapped.

Cam refused to snap back. "I meant car or Casper trouble." And there had definitely been Casper trouble, poor dog. Cam was beginning to wonder if the food had gone bad and Casper had taken one for the team.

Zoey threw a look over her shoulder. "He's got to be empty by now. Kate said not to feed him for the rest of the day. And he's not dehydrated—she told me how to check."

"Zoey, you've got to admit that he's more comfortable in the car than he'd be in his crate on an airplane. Gaining three hours in the middle of the night didn't seem worth putting him through the stress."

"I still can't believe driving— What did you say, eighteen hours? I can't believe with that long a drive, we'd only get to Ellensburg three hours later than if we flew."

"See, it's because we're not going all the way to Seattle.

If you flew, you'd have to drive a couple of hours to get to the kennel. When you consider that and—"

"I know," Zoey broke in. "The flight schedule, blah blah, landing at night, blah blah, getting luggage, renting car, blah blah. I heard you the first two times you mentioned it to me." She stared out the window.

The decision to drive had made sense to him and he'd honestly assumed she'd agree after he explained. But if anything, Zoey was angrier than ever.

Something else was going on here. "Why are you so angry?"

"Because you made the decision without asking me."

Fair enough. "You were asleep and I didn't want to disturb you, especially because I expected you to agree. But you're right. I should have discussed driving the rest of the way with you first."

"Thank you."

Cam waited, but her demeanor didn't change. She didn't even look at him. He hoped he wasn't going to have to offer to go to Denver after all. "There's more, though. What?"

"I *stressed* how important it is that I do this myself!" she burst out. "I really want to get Casper to the kennel, let him do his thing and deliver him back home safely. I have to do this on my own because if I succeed, maybe it'll end the Zoey disaster jinx."

"So you're saying that because we're driving directly to the kennel, it somehow doesn't count?"

She sighed. "I've depended on you too much. You got me food in Chicago, you helped take care of Casper, you got us the cars, you've researched flights—you've pretty much taken over and I've just gone along for the ride."

And it had been a great ride. "We teamed up. You watched my samples for me. Otherwise, I would have had to lug that box all over the place. And the only reason

Joyce let us use her car was because you and Casper were with me. There's no way she would have let a strange man drive her to the wedding."

"She Googled us."

"She wouldn't have bothered to even do that without you and Casper."

"Okay," Zoey said. "Getting to Des Moines was a joint effort, but then you didn't get on a plane. You stayed behind to help me. And I let you."

"So? It's called using your available resources—me. That's not cheating. That's smart. You don't get extra points for making things difficult for yourself."

"But…if you hadn't helped me, what would have happened?"

"You would have managed. Casper would have spent a lot more hours in his crate and you would have spent a lot more hours standing in line. Whether Casper showed up for his rendezvous on time would have been totally out of your hands. Same with me and my meeting. But we didn't let some random ticket agent decide our fate. We took control. We chose to act."

"It's the choosing to act part that usually bites me in the butt," she muttered.

Memories of her turquoise panties floated through Cam's mind.

"Oh, for pity's sake!" She threw her hands up. "I know what you're thinking."

He grinned and she responded with a small smile—a very small smile. But it was a start. "At least if you fail, if *we* fail, we can say we tried to succeed instead of doing nothing and failing anyway."

"Hmm." She appeared to consider what he'd said. "Did you make that up, or is it from some speech you had to memorize in school?"

"My high school football coach may have said something similar once, and if he didn't, he should have. I remember he did used to say 'It's better to try and fail than fail to try.'"

Zoey shook her head. "You make driving for hours seem so reasonable, but the fact is you made the decision without me. Why? Do you believe I'm incapable of making a good decision?"

Cam ran through his list of swearing numbers. He'd hoped to avoid this. "If you want to go to Denver, I'll drive you to Denver."

"But we passed the turnoff hours ago!"

Cam reached into the back for his laptop and handed it to her just as his phone buzzed. "We can be there in an hour and a half. I downloaded flight schedules. Call and check what's available."

He stared at his phone. Gus. Again. "What's up, Gus?"

"You tell me." Cam heard absolutely no trace of an accent in Gus's voice, which meant he was extremely angry about something, or more likely *at someone,* probably Cam.

Everybody was mad at Cam today.

"I'm parked on the side of the road in Wyoming trying to figure out my next move. You?"

"You might have given me a heads up that we were going to have visitors."

"Who?" He hadn't forgotten an appointment, had he?

"Bunch of infernal Campbells poking their noses into everything."

A bunch of… "Richard sent his people to check out the brewery?"

"Aye."

What was Richard up to? "How many?"

"Even one is too many."

"Gus. I didn't know Richard was going to do that. I haven't met with the guy yet. Who did he send?"

"There is a lawyer type and a bean counter and a man who claims to know a thing or two about brewing. Then there's a slick fella who has no discernible function other than to stare at everybody with his beady little Campbell eyes."

"They're not really all named Campbell, are they, Gus?"

"Might as well be. That's where their loyalty lies. Hey! You with the fancy computer thing—you can't go in there."

Cam couldn't hear the reply, but he heard Gus. "I don't care if they are. You keep your grimy Campbell hands off my assets!"

"Gus?"

"They say they have a right to look at the recipes."

"Not yet, they don't."

"Not ever as long as there's a breath in my body!"

"Gus, calm down. Richard probably asked his finance guy to check us out to make sure we wouldn't take his money and disappear. They're just being overzealous. Explain that Richard and I have yet to meet and invite them to return when and if we reach a preliminary agreement."

"With pleasure." Before the connection ended, Cam heard, "Be off, ye Campbell wankers! And don't come back until ye show me the color of your money!"

Cam winced.

"I heard that all the way over here." Zoey was struggling not to laugh.

"Gus can be…Gus."

"He's your cousin. The red-headed one?"

Cam nodded. "The one who forgot he told you that you could take the beer out of the cooler."

"I remember him. He's very…colorful."

Cam considered Gus. "He's a hard worker," he said and

was surprised to realize it was true. "But his contributions are more…abstract, I guess. I'm not sure exactly what it is he does, but he does it very well."

"Gus is your brand," Zoey said. "Like what Joyce recommended to me for my Skin Garden line. It's not enough to make a fabulous product. You also have to identify your market and sell it to them. The customer wants an experience along with the product. And your product must provide something no one else's does. Gus is your 'something.'"

"He is that." Cam tried to imagine MacNeil's without Gus and couldn't. Cam was fine with people when he had to be, but Gus was a natural. People were drawn to him and thus drawn to the beer with his picture on the label. So it wasn't all about Gus's enormous ego.

"That day he made me laugh," Zoey was saying. "He made me feel like we were going to throw the best party ever. And we did. People still remember it."

"I know *I* remember it." Cam nudged her shoulder when she immediately looked stricken. "Stop it. It's funny. And Gus has told the exploding beer story a hundred times."

Zoey appeared so horrified that Cam burst into deep, soul-cleansing laughter.

Casper barked at him and that made Cam laugh more. Finally Zoey joined him.

"Look! I'm crying." She sniffed and dug in her purse for a tissue. "I don't know why I'm laughing." She dabbed her eyes. "I'm in a car by the side of the road in Wyoming in the dead of winter with a crazy man and a dog with intestinal issues."

"Because you're a saint, Zoey."

"And *this* is my reward?"

That set them off again, which got Casper all riled up, so they both got out of the car and walked him.

Cam inhaled the clean, cold air and viewed the stark beauty of the distant mountains against one of the bluest skies he'd ever seen.

And then he looked down at the woman standing next to him, wearing the silly candy-cane hat, and emotion clogged his throat. He couldn't imagine the brewery without Gus and he couldn't imagine the rest of his life without Zoey.

He drew another breath. "I have to say something." His heart thumped. *Too soon. Too soon. Too soon.* "I love you."

The words hung in the air. Cam didn't look at Zoey because he'd want to see answering love in her eyes, and he knew it wouldn't be there. Not yet. "That's a big part of why I didn't go to the airport. I wasn't ready to say goodbye to you. So I convinced myself that driving straight through was better than gambling that you could get a flight today. I was selfish. Can you forgive me?"

He risked a glance at her. There was something in her eyes. He couldn't call it love, but it was something.

"You make the best apologies." Her voice was a gruff whisper. She cleared her throat. "Yes, you're forgiven. Especially since there are only two possible flights and neither airline would accept a reservation for Casper until the weather conditions are confirmed nearer to departure."

She gave him a wry smile and surprised him with a quick, cold kiss. "The road trip is *on*."

13

HE'D SAID THE *L* WORD.

Incredibly, this great, heart-meltingly sexy man had told Zoey he loved her.

And even more incredibly, she hadn't said it back.

It wasn't because she didn't love him. It was because once she said the words, Cam would take on all her problems as his own. That's the kind of person he was. When he committed, he was all in, one hundred percent, accepting the good and the bad. Before Zoey could let him do that, she had to make sure there wasn't too much bad for him to accept.

She didn't want Cam solving her problems; she wanted to take care of them on her own. Besides, there would be plenty of problems that belonged to both of them in the future. If she and Cam got together, she wanted to add to the relationship instead of immediately taking from it.

She had to protect Cam from himself.

As if Kate's pregnancy hadn't already raised the stakes on getting Casper to Merriweather Kennels, Zoey wanted to demonstrate to Cam that she wasn't a total incompetent.

No matter what he said, Zoey knew he didn't have total confidence in her. But why would Cam believe that

Zoey could do this on her own when she herself wasn't completely convinced she could? From the moment she'd agreed to help her sister, Zoey hadn't truly believed she could pull it off. She'd expected failure. It wasn't a matter of if, but when.

Cam had given her hope. And he was right. A win was a win. It didn't have to be pretty.

They climbed into the car. Casper seemed perky, drank water and appeared to be over his Chinese food–induced tummy ache.

Even his paws looked great. Zoey had slathered them with one of her skin-soothing balms and used the same conditioner she used on her own hair on the ends of his coat.

She had all sorts of special dog-grooming products in the suitcase but nothing that repelled the dirty slush Casper had walked through the past several days. Though she'd regularly cleaned his legs and paws, the hair only got dingier. But the skin soothing balm was doing the trick, and as a bonus, Casper had stopped licking and chewing his paws.

She finished making sure he was dry before they started on the long slog to Washington and conditioned the outer layer of his coat just for grins. Besides, it helped get rid of the wet dog smell that permeated the car.

Zoey climbed out of the back, walked around to the driver's side and opened the door. "Out, MacNeil. I'm driving."

Cam stood. "Do you know where you're going?"

Zoey pointed. "That way."

Cam laughed, and when he got into the passenger seat, he opened his laptop and showed her the map.

"Wow. We really are right above Denver."

"You can still head for the airport," he said. "Your call."

"No. This feels right. Besides, Denver isn't the only

airport around. I notice we're going by Salt Lake City and then there's Boise after that. If we don't like driving in the dark, we can pick another airport." There. A plan. With options, even.

"Absolutely," Cam said heartily.

"Dial it down, MacNeil. Or learn to fake it better."

"Okay." He didn't seem bothered that she'd caught him. "Don't count on the other airports. They're too small. You'll probably just be routed back to Denver for a connecting flight."

"Ugh." Zoey sighed and started the car. "You don't have to dial it down *that* much."

"We've got a few hours' cushion, unless you want to land on the kennel's doorstep at four in the morning. So if we have to, we can stop to rest for a while and still get there in plenty of time."

Noted, but Zoey didn't intend to stop until Casper was at the kennel. "As long as you can still get to your meeting. What's the latest you can leave Merriweather after dropping me off?"

"Eight-thirty," he answered after a brief pause.

Zoey bet that pause meant he should actually leave closer to eight o'clock and silently planned on making sure he was able to take off by then.

She pulled back onto the highway and settled in. "So Cam, I've been wondering—why are we getting a better cell connection on a Wyoming highway than I get in my apartment?"

CAM GOT THE message loud and clear.

He'd known it was too early to tell her he loved her, and although he hadn't expected to hear it back—well, he'd hoped—he had expected her to say *something*.

But she'd totally ignored what was a huge milestone in

any relationship. Instead, she'd taken two giant emotional steps backward, and now they were talking cell-phone reception as though they were a couple of strangers.

Awkward.

But when one person says, "I love you" and the other doesn't, how can it be anything but awkward?

Okay, he'd admit it. He *had* counted on hearing, "Oh, Cam, I love you, too!" and Zoey falling into his arms. Now he had sixteen more hours of awkwardness to get through and it was his own fault. Sixteen more hours of making conversation about nothing or pretending to sleep.

Pretending to sleep sounded more appealing than discussing the weird cloud formations in the sky ahead of them, as they were doing now.

Cam closed his eyes and heard Zoey sigh.

The car slowed.

He opened his eyes. "What's wrong?"

"You're acting weird because I didn't tell you that I loved you, too."

She pulled over to the side of the road and shut off the car, just when Cam had accepted that discussing those three little words was off the table.

Fine. "I didn't tell you I loved you just so you'd say it back, but you didn't say anything at all."

"Because I didn't want *you* to say anything yet!"

Yet. Cam heard that.

She continued, "You were saying you'd really be there for me, as though you *expect* to have to rescue me. I want you to expect that I *won't* need rescuing."

"Got it." At least he hoped he did. "No rescuing."

"I mean it," Zoey insisted.

"So do I. I couldn't rescue you even if I wanted to. I'll be at the farm with Richard. But I wanted you to know I'd love you even if you did need rescuing."

"But I won't."

"Okay."

"Okay."

They stared at each other. Zoey didn't restart the car.

"Are we good?" he asked.

"Will you take it back?"

Cam looked her right in her sea-green eyes. "No."

She smiled. "We're good."

ZOEY PARKED THE car and exhaled. "We're here." She'd done it, at least the important part. Not that getting Casper home safely wasn't important, too, but she was going to savor this moment.

"Congratulations." Cam appeared genuinely pleased for her.

She was glad he understood. Zoey had insisted on doing most of the driving and he hadn't argued with her. He'd even slept some.

That showed he trusted her, didn't it?

And now she was here, with Casper, a dozen steps away from the Merriweather Kennel's door—not to be confused with the front door of the elegant house attached to the kennel.

She breathed deeply. "So this is what success feels like."

"It's great, isn't it?" Cam stretched. "I hope to experience the feeling myself this morning."

"You will. Remember, sometimes ya gotta walk."

"So you're quoting me to me now?" Cam laughed.

"If the quote fits…" She was aware that Cam wanted an infusion of cash to lighten his load at the brewery, and she understood she was now part of that reason. But she didn't want him to agree to a bad deal.

"I won't be stupid, Zoey. Don't worry."

"I'm not worried."

"Great. Neither am I."

They got out of the car. "Wait a sec," she said.

Cam stood to the side while Zoey took a picture of the kennel entrance and sent it to Kate. She'd also taken a picture of the entrance gate off the highway and sent that to her sister, which had prompted a squealing phone call from Kate that was cut short because she and Ryan had been about to board a plane for their flight home.

To be honest, Zoey was glad that Kate wouldn't be able to talk to her because she half-expected Kate to want to be on the phone with her while Casper did his thing.

A beeping sounded. "Oops. There went the battery." She dropped the phone into her pocket. "I'll have to remember to find someplace to recharge it."

Cam helped her unload the luggage and Casper's crate. They could hear dogs barking in the early morning. Casper was sniffing the air and behaving perfectly. Zoey supposed his dog show training had kicked in.

She'd called Martha last night and warned her that they'd be arriving early. She and Cam had even had time for breakfast and a gallon of coffee. She'd also reassembled the now slightly diminished gift basket of her products for Martha and brushed Casper.

He looked handsome.

And so did Cam, with his dark stubble and slightly messed up hair.

He loved her. He'd told her so.

And she loved him. She had not told him so.

But she would. If all went well, maybe sooner rather than later.

Cam set Casper's suitcase by her feet and drew his hands to his waist. "Well," he said and smiled down at her. Zoey almost, *almost* threw her arms around him and shouted that she loved him, too.

She forced herself to be patient a while longer. "Well," she said. Goodbye was stuck in her throat.

"I'll call—"

"Best of luck with—"

They broke off and laughed. "So you're staying overnight, yes?" Cam asked. "I just want to make sure before I leave you here."

Zoey nodded. "They've got a guest room for this very situation."

"I'll stop by on my way back to Seattle. Not to check up on you or anything, but I'd like to tell you about my meeting with Richard." Then he showed those dimples of his. "And if you want to report on how Casper and his lady friend are getting along, it would be nice to hear that, too."

"Call first," she warned, even though his dimples were very persuasive.

"Absolutely."

He gazed intently at her, and Zoey remembered other times he'd looked at her that way and what had happened shortly after...

She gasped. "What are we doing standing here? You should go!"

"I've got plenty of time." Cam reached for her. "I'll get there by nine or nine-fifteen."

Zoey nodded and stepped into his arms. They held each other for a few minutes, saying everything that needed saying without words. That was a good thing because Zoey's throat was really tight. For pity's sake, she wasn't going to *cry,* was she?

Cam tilted her chin and gave her a hot kiss that dissolved into a tenderness that made Zoey's heart melt.

He drew back and gave her a scorching look, well aware that he wasn't playing fair.

"Later," she whispered, stepping away.

Cam stooped to pat Casper before getting into the car. "Remember to romance her a little first, okay, buddy? She'll be putty in your paws."

"Cam!" Laughing, Zoey waved him away, watching until he flashed his taillights and turned onto the highway.

Casper whined.

"Yeah. I miss him, too."

A door opened behind her. "What an attractive male," she heard a woman say.

"Yes. He's my boyfriend," Zoey said, trying out the term. It didn't seem adequate.

The woman laughed. "I meant your dog. But the guy wasn't bad, either."

Zoey laughed, a little embarrassed. "I'm Zoey Archer and this is Casper. Are you Martha?"

The woman shook her head as she approached Zoey. "I'm Sheryl. I'm one of the handlers."

"Martha is expecting us. We're here to, um, well, Casper is here to make puppies." Could she sound any prissier? "I apologize for showing up so early, but I know timing is an issue."

"Not a problem. I'm actually about to leave. Martha is in the kennel and will be out in a minute." She gestured to the leash. "Do you mind if I…?"

"Go ahead."

Zoey surrendered the leash and Sheryl walked Casper several feet away. With a few softly worded commands, they trotted around an imaginary show ring.

As she watched Casper's elegant trot, Zoey understood why her sister and brother-in-law loved showing and raising dogs, and this breed in particular.

Casper was gorgeous. With his long nose and aristocratic air, he looked sleekly sophisticated His coat shone in the morning sun, and, yes, Zoey was going to take credit for that. She loved the way it moved and rippled.

Sheryl came to a stop. "Does he self stack?"

"Huh?"

She said something and Casper assumed the position, as Zoey thought of it. Sheryl knelt and ran her hands over him and Casper didn't flinch.

What a pro. Zoey smiled to herself as she remembered the wet dog zooming between rooms in the motel.

Sheryl gave Casper a final pat and stood. "What a wonderful dog." There was a touch of surprise in her voice.

Guess they didn't know just how great Casper was. Zoey would have to remember to tell Kate.

She glanced sharply at Zoey. "You are aware this dog could give Alexandra a run for her money?"

Zoey wasn't sure how to respond. "This is my sister's dog. I just brought him here for her. But I'll pass along your comments."

"She's not a breeder then?"

"Oh, yes. Ryka Kennels in Virginia."

"Virginia." Sheryl stared at Casper. "I've heard of them. They're fairly new at this, aren't they?"

"Three or four years, I believe."

"And siring Merriweather puppies will quickly enhance their reputation." She nodded to herself and then smiled quickly at Zoey. "Let's hope it works out for them." The way she spoke sounded as though she doubted it would.

What was that about? Before Zoey could ask, Sheryl reached for her suitcase. "Let me help you carry in your things, and then I have to get going."

Hoisting her backpack over her shoulder, Zoey put the gift basket inside Casper's crate and brought it and Casper into the kennel offices.

The first thing that greeted Zoey was a huge painting

of Alexandra of Thebes anchoring a display that covered an entire wall.

"Wow," Zoey said. Because, well, wow.

"You've never seen her in person?" Sheryl asked.

Zoey shook her head.

"I'd put her through her paces for you now, but we're trying to keep her calm."

"I understand," Zoey said.

"Well, it was lovely to meet you and Casper, and I'll let Martha know you're here," Sheryl said.

Zoey took her gift basket out of the crate and set it on a console table in the little sitting area as though she was leaving a tribute at the altar of Alexandra of Thebes.

She surveyed the room, noting that other Merriweather champions had also been featured. "Hey, Casper, check it out. You'll have a wall like this someday." Ribbons and photographs covered every possible bit of wall space in the sitting area, as well as the office she could see into and the long hallway leading in both directions. A bookcase held giant scrapbooks. The overflow pictures, Zoey guessed.

But of course the wall visitors saw first upon entering was Alexandra's. The photographs from the dog shows all looked the same to Zoey. She enjoyed the puppy pictures best. Merriweather had kept two other puppies from the same litter as Alexandra, Cleopatra of Thebes and Rameses of Thebes. Like Casper, Rameses had the CH in front of his name, designating a champion, and had what would have been an impressive bunch of ribbons if they hadn't been displayed next to his sister's.

But the other dog, although she appeared in lots of pictures with Alexandra and was the mirror image of her, had only a couple of ribbons. "Oooh, poor Cleopatra," Zoey murmured aloud. "Living in the shadow of your perfect sister. Been there, done that."

A door opened at the end of the hallway and a woman approached Zoey and Casper. The woman was tall with brown eyes and a thin face. She wore her shoulder-length gray hair parted in the middle. Zoey's eyes widened and she wished Cam were here. He'd get a kick out of this woman who looked as though she could be Casper's distant relative.

"Oh, what a pretty boy!"

Naturally, she greeted Casper first. She stooped and ran her hands over him, getting personal really fast.

If Zoey's eyes hadn't already been wide from the woman's appearance, they would have widened at this.

"I'm Martha Merriweather." Standing, she offered her hand to Zoey, who tried not to think about where that hand had just been. Dog people. Sheesh.

"Zoey Archer. I'm Kate's sister. She's very sorry—" *understatement* "—that she couldn't be here, but she and her husband were at a wedding in Costa Rica."

"Yes, she told me. Aren't you a special sister for bringing Casper here for her?"

Zoey smiled, although she didn't much like the sound of the word "special."

"Have you eaten breakfast? May I get you some coffee?" Martha asked.

"I'm fine," Zoey assured her.

"All right." She gestured. "Come with me and we'll let these two get acquainted. I'll show you where you can leave your things afterward. Normally, I wouldn't be so abrupt, but we've left this a little late."

Zoey led Casper down the "Gallery of Champions," as designated by a plaque in the hallway.

"Do you work at the kennel?" Martha asked.

Zoey shook her head. Surely Kate had mentioned that Zoey was a total novice.

"Do you live nearby? Visit often?"

Again, Zoey shook her head.

"But you must share your sister's love of the breed." Martha wasn't asking, but Zoey got the impression she expected an answer, and it had better be one she wanted to hear.

"Just not her experience." All parties needed to be clear on that. What did it matter whether Zoey was a nut about Afghan hounds? She liked Casper. That was enough.

Martha led them to the indoor–outdoor kennel runs, laid out in long rows. Ryka had a similar setup but on a much smaller scale. "I'm going to put Casper in Cleo's run. It's right next to Alexandra's. We'll introduce them to each other slowly before we let them into the larger play area."

Only one dog was in the kennel, a magnificent white creature that could have been Casper's twin. Casper perked up, sniffing eagerly. She backed up against the metal fencing separating the runs.

"Where are the other dogs?" Zoey asked.

"Oh," Martha gave a little stressed sigh as she opened the door to the run. "Some are being groomed and some are at shows, and we've moved the others to the side exercise yard. We don't want these two to get distracted."

"I don't think Casper will be distracted."

Casper had leapt into the run and was moving back and forth trying to find a way to get to Alexandra, who looked at him with wary disdain.

Zoey couldn't help comparing him to an inexperienced freshman putting the moves on the head cheerleader.

Casper flung himself at the fencing and Zoey winced. Alexandra snarled.

"That doesn't look good," Zoey said.

"It'll be a different story once she decides she's ready."

Alexandra lunged and snapped. Casper jumped away.

"They just need to get used to each other," Martha said. "It might take a day or two."

"Do we have a day or two?" Zoey had assumed she'd barely made it in time.

"Nature will take over eventually," Martha said, which didn't exactly answer Zoey's question. "Meanwhile, do you have some papers for me?"

"Yes. They're in the suitcase." Kate had scanned Casper's medical history and lineage and had already emailed them to Martha, but the other woman wanted hard copies. "Oh, and I brought you a gift." Some of Joyce's advice about branding and packaging floated through Zoey's mind. "They're samples from my organic skin-care line. I know when you work around dogs you don't want to use any product that could irritate their skin or eyes or make them sick if they ingest it. My products are all natural. I don't put anything in them that you couldn't eat." *Target marketing. Was she on fire, or what?* And if Martha asked, she'd point to Casper's coat, which was way shinier than Alexandra's, and mention that she'd used her own hair conditioner on it. Except she'd used up the sample she'd intended to put in the basket.

"That sounds lovely," Martha said without taking her gaze from the two dogs.

Her products would speak for themselves, Zoey told herself as she made her way back down the long, award-filled hallway to the kennel reception area.

Zoey took a moment to peer into some of the other rooms; Kate would ask about Merriweather's setup. She saw one room that was clearly used for medical care. It reminded Zoey of a school nurse's office. Another looked like a day care, and Zoey imagined prospective owners and puppies bonding there. And then she passed the nursery with padded boxes surrounded by a low barrier that would let mama dogs out and keep puppies in. The whole place seemed first rate and clean, as it should.

When she got to the reception area, Zoey carried her suitcase, backpack and Casper's crate into the office to get them out of the way, but she decided to leave the gift basket sitting on the console table. As she turned around, she noticed a cabinet by the front door that contained dog-grooming supplies bearing the Merriweather label.

Oops. It would have been awkward if she'd pointed out how shiny Casper's coat was compared to Alexandra's. But she'd definitely mention it to Kate. And maybe Zoey could develop a dog-grooming line for Ryka! How perfect would that be?

As she returned to the kennel runs, papers in hand, Zoey felt light and happy for the first time in…forever. Things were finally going her way. She was confident and full of possibilities for Skin Garden, and she'd met Cam.

Cam. She stopped and closed her eyes as emotion washed over her. At first, she'd thought he was too good to be true, but now she realized she'd believed he was too good for *her*.

She didn't want to believe that. She didn't like believing that. Success would change how she saw herself.

As soon as she got home to Texas—no, as soon as she got on the plane in Richmond…actually, as soon as Zoey brought Casper back to Ryka, she was going to call Cam and tell him she loved him. She wouldn't even get out of the car first.

Zoey practically floated the rest of the way down the hall, imagining scenarios of Cam waiting for her at the airport in Austin and running into his arms just like in the movies.

"Cleo—stop it!"

The words brought Zoey down to earth.

The tone registered first. She was used to hearing the quiet, firm voice the trainers and handlers adopted when working with dogs, the one she'd tried to emulate but not always successfully.

"Sit! Cleo! Get back here!"

To hear Martha lose it was just…just unthinkable.

So was a dog who wouldn't obey, especially a dog who had a whole alphabet soup of championship designations in front of her name.

Her name. Martha had called the dog Cleo. She'd been speaking to Cleo, Alexandra's failure of a sister. She must have escaped from wherever they'd been keeping her and run back to the kennel.

No wonder she was a failure if that's the way they talked to her all the time.

Like Kate talks to you.

Zoey shook the thought away. That was in the past, but she still felt a whole lot of sympathy for poor Cleo.

"Sit!"

The harshly worded command made Zoey flinch. She pushed open the door, deciding she'd give Cleo some love. There was Casper, still panting eagerly. Martha, who shot a quick glance over her shoulder when Zoey came in, was now in the other run holding onto a squirming dog's collar.

That would be Cleo. Wow. To Zoey, she looked exactly like her sister, but there must be some crucial difference that made one an überchampion and the other a nobody.

Zoey scanned the room for Alexandra, hoping to see the two sisters together before they dragged Cleo away. But there was only one other dog in the room besides Casper.

"Where's…" She trailed off. Something was wrong. All the little niggling things she'd ignored or dismissed as dog-people quirkiness returned.

The strange reaction of Sheryl, the woman who'd

greeted her. Kate's stunned surprise at Casper being invited to breed with the great Alexandra of Thebes.

And that was another thing. Zoey had expected to be blown away when she first saw Alexandra in person, but she wasn't. This was Merriweather's star, their queen. She'd have been pampered within an inch of her life. No one would yell at her because no one would have to. Even if her personality changed because she had doggie PMS or something, they'd coddle her.

She observed Casper, trying to claw his way through the barrier that kept him from a female in heat—the female Martha was trying to calm.

He had a silkier coat. How could a dog who'd been traveling for days, who'd romped through dirty, slushy snow and had been washed in a motel bathtub look better than the best Afghan hound in the country?

Even if she weren't show ready, Alexandra should look better than the dog Martha was petting. The dog she'd called Cleo.

"Where's what?" Martha asked.

Alexandra. The dog who we're supposed to be breeding with Casper. "A restroom I could use."

Was that relief on Martha's face? "There's a public restroom near the front office. You can leave the papers there, too."

Zoey barely heard her. She murmured something and retreated into the hallway. Now what?

14

CAM HAD STOPPED in Ellensburg to get gas and clean up before driving on to Mabton. Zoey had helped him arrange the beer in the presentation box, so that was done. He allowed himself to think of her one last time before changing his focus to the upcoming meeting.

He'd shaved, changed his shirt and now stared at himself in the restroom mirror. He looked tense. He shouldn't look tense. He shouldn't *be* tense. But he was.

Cam moved his shoulders around and tried to channel a little of Gus's casual amiability. Not too much, or he'd come across as fake, and nothing seemed more desperate than obviously fake casualness.

He wasn't desperate; he just wanted this a whole lot.

Cam spread his arms wide, as he'd seen Gus do a million times, and quickly dropped them. That was horrible.

Shaking his head, he shrugged into his jacket and picked up his bag just as his cell buzzed.

Gus. Cam pushed open the restroom door. He'd wanted to channel Gus, not talk with him.

"You're up early," Cam said.

"Have you had your meeting with him yet?" Gus asked.

"No." Cam didn't have to ask who.

"Cancel."

"No."

"You don't need his money, Cam. Someone has made an offer on those tanks at the Beer Barn."

Cam abruptly stopped walking. "Who?"

"They won't say."

"Cash?"

"Apparently so. They've asked if we want to counter."

"How much?"

Gus barked a laugh. "More than we've got."

Which was the point of meeting with Richard. "I need a number, Gus."

"It'll just depress you. Tell you what. I'll be seeing the lads tomorrow and we'll have a little chat after they've cleaned up from the tour." Gus chuckled. "They'll be much more agreeable to kicking in money to hire some college kids to help you out."

Gus still wouldn't admit that Cam required more than a few hours a week from college kids, but Cam wasn't going to argue with him now. "Sounds like a plan. Listen, I'm heading out to the farm. I'll talk with you later."

Cam checked his watch. He wanted to call the owner of the Beer Barn, but it was five-thirty in the morning there. Maybe he'd have an opportunity to try later.

He was stowing his bag in the SUV when a motor home pulled up to the gas tanks. *Merriweather Kennels* was painted on the side, along with the portrait of an Afghan dog that looked just like Casper. *Alexandra* was arched in quotes above the picture and beneath it was what Cam figured was her official name, prefaced by a bunch of letters that reminded him of the initials that trailed doctors' and lawyers' names. They seemed proud of them, but nobody outside the profession knew exactly what they meant.

Zoey had said the dog was hot stuff and she must be if she got to travel around in her own motor home.

A man got out and started pumping gas. Moments later, a woman emerged from the side door followed by a white dog in a navy-blue coat and hood embroidered with "Merriweather's Cleopatra of Thebes."

"She's antsy," he heard the woman say. "I'll walk her around."

Cam watched them jog in that trot Zoey had used with Casper, but he could tell the woman was much more practiced than Zoey. When they came within a few feet of him, Cam said, "They're beautiful dogs." He couldn't help smiling as he added, "I've recently become quite a fan."

"This one will make a fan out of anyone." The woman smiled at him. "Would you like her autograph?"

"I—what?"

She laughed and took a card from her pocket. "I always carry these when I'm with her."

It was a smaller version of the picture on the side of the motor home, but this one had a paw print with *Alexandra* in a loopy script.

How often had Cam heard that name in the past few days? "I've heard a lot about her. I was hoping to get to see her."

"And here she is!" The woman gazed proudly at the dog.

Wait a minute. Cam had been about to explain about bringing Casper to the kennel. "You mean here? Now? This is Alexandra?"

"Yes." The woman nodded, misinterpreting his stunned expression. "This is *the* Alexandra of Thebes."

"Wow. I—I thought she was at the kennel."

"We just left there."

Left? That was quick. If he'd known, he would have waited for Zoey.

"Were you going there today to see Alexandra?" the woman asked.

"I'd hoped to. I have another stop first."

"You're lucky you caught us here. You would have missed her otherwise, and you'll never meet another Afghan hound as fine as she is. I'm sorry I can't take her coat off for you, but I'll show her if you'd like."

"That'd be great." Cam watched as the handler paraded the dog back and forth.

"She has more Grand Champion points than any other Afghan hound in the country," the woman informed him when they came to a stop and she positioned the tail to curl over the dog's back.

Honestly? Coat or not, Cam couldn't see much difference between Casper and this dog.

"She's going to get more points next week, aren't you, pretty girl?" She rubbed the dog's hooded head.

"At the big show?" Cam asked.

"The Moorefield, yes. Are you going to be there?"

"Unfortunately, no." Cam didn't know anything about the dog show or where it was, but he remembered Zoey saying that Casper was going to be there. She'd also said that Alexandra *wasn't* going to be there, giving Casper a good chance of winning.

"You should really try. I'm not sure how much longer Martha will continue to show her, but by the time she retires, Alexandra will have more points than any other dog of *any* breed." The woman spoke reverently. "The ultimate Grand Champion."

"Could I take a video while you walk her again?" He whipped out his phone. "If I end up buying one of these dogs, I want to remember what the very best looks like. Has she ever had puppies?"

"Oh, don't set your sights there." The woman gave him

a patronizing stare. "They'll only go to professionals, and there is already a waiting list."

"Probably out of my price range, too." Cam held up his phone while the woman trotted with Alexandra. "Why does her coat say Cleopatra? Is that her official name?"

"Oh." The woman stopped and glanced down. "I didn't notice. Cleo is her littermate and travels with her."

"Is she a show dog, too?" Cam lowered his phone but kept recording.

The woman shook her head. "Regrettably, no. That dog doesn't have the temperament, but Alexandra shows much better when Cleo is with her. Cleo keeps her calm. Alexandra hasn't lost since we started keeping the two of them together."

"She's not with her now?" Cam peered around, looking for yet another large, white, showy dog.

"No. She's in season and is being bred. The last time we bred Cleo, it upset Alexandra so." She reached down and stroked the dog. "And with the show next week, we don't want her to get agitated."

"Why would she be upset?"

"All the dogs are upset at the way Cleo carries on. She's a real bitch in every possible way." The woman lowered her voice. "She bit the last stud."

"Ouch." Cam involuntarily moved his hand to cover his own studly parts.

"That was so unfortunate." The woman sucked her breath between her teeth. "She panicked during the tie and, well, let's just say it was very costly, both financially and because it's been impossible to find any breeder willing to risk a quality stud with her."

Cam started to sweat. Hours ago, he wouldn't have had a clue what the term "tie" meant, though he could have guessed.

"Because of the biting?" he asked.

"That and the other injury."

Cam felt himself shrivel. "What other injury?"

The woman hesitated, belatedly wary. "I'd rather not go into details." She shortened Alexandra's leash.

"I would. I want to go into details."

"Sheryl!" The man waved her over.

"It's time for us to leave." She trotted Alexandra over to the motor home.

Cam followed.

The woman yanked open the door. "Up," she ordered the dog.

"Sheryl?" Cam tried to appear nonthreatening when he wanted to choke the information out of her. "The...the other dog didn't die, did he?" Cam couldn't believe how hard his heart was pounding—not only for Zoey, but for Casper, too. Who would have figured?

"Oh, no." She shook her head. "No, no. But he was unable to perform after that. I can assure you, though, the stud's owners were generously compensated for the unfortunate accident."

If Cam were injured to the point where he couldn't "perform," it would be a hell of a lot more than "unfortunate."

Then Sheryl obviously remembered that she was supposedly talking to a potential buyer. "I guarantee that Merriweather Kennels is a first-rate breeding facility and we've taken steps to ensure that an incident like that won't happen again. In fact, if you're looking for a dog to show, Cleo's puppies will have impeccable bloodlines."

"But not Grand Champion bloodlines."

She shook her head. "No." She stepped away, eyeing him carefully. "But don't discount the importance of temperament and training."

Cam deliberately relaxed his posture and smiled his

you-sexy-thing smile, even though it probably didn't come off very convincingly. "Thanks so much for talking with me. I've learned a lot." He held up a hand and backed toward the SUV. "Good luck."

Why had he said *that?* It appeared Merriweather Kennels made its own luck.

He didn't even close the car door before aiming his phone at the motor home for some final video as it drove off. Then he punched in Zoey's number.

His call immediately went to voice mail. The batteries. She must not have plugged in the phone yet. Cam tried twice more to make sure, and then searched for the kennel's number.

When someone finally answered, he started to ask for Zoey but changed his mind and asked for Martha Merriweather. He didn't want Zoey to have to leave Casper—if she was with him—and he instinctively knew Martha wasn't going to leave her dog alone with Casper.

Or had that been her plan all along? Take out the competition? Palm off Cleopatra's puppies as Alexandra's? *It's been impossible to find any breeder willing to risk a quality stud with her.*

Any breeder who knew the story. Cam bet Zoey's sister didn't. And anyway, if she did, she would have believed Casper was breeding with Alexandra.

"I'm sorry," said a voice in his ear. "Mrs. Merriweather is unable to come to the phone. May I have her return your call? Or is there something I could help you with?"

"Does she have a cell phone?"

"Not with her. She prefers not to be disturbed while working with the dogs."

Cam didn't want to leave a warning message for Zoey with a kennel employee. "I'll call back later," he said and dropped his head to the steering wheel.

It'll be okay, he told himself. Zoey could handle it. She was watching Casper, and obviously Martha Merriweather was highly motivated to make certain there wasn't a repeat of Cleo's last breeding attempt.

Cam started the car and pulled onto the highway toward the hops farm. Was it possible that Zoey's sister had misunderstood? Anyway, if Casper did breed with the wrong dog, that was between the two owners. It wasn't his responsibility. It wasn't even Zoey's responsibility. She'd delivered the dog. She'd done her part. She'd succeeded.

But what if Casper were injured right in front of her? What if *Zoey* were injured trying to protect Casper?

Cam wanted to warn her. Warning her wasn't the same as helping, was it?

But if he went back to the kennel now, he wouldn't be able to meet with Richard, and from what Gus had told him, Richard had more in mind than having a beer named after him. It sounded as though Richard wanted to take over. That couldn't be right. Cam really needed to meet with him.

But could he live with himself if Zoey were hurt? Was the brewery more important than her safety?

No.

And that's when Cam turned the car around.

As Zoey reentered the kennel area, she still hadn't decided what to do.

Martha was waiting for her. The runs were empty and the barrier behind the doggie doors to the outside had been raised.

"Where are the dogs?" she asked.

Martha gestured for Zoey to follow her. "I let them into the small play yard together. If they get along and she indicates a willingness to stand, then we'll bring them back inside and let Casper try to mount her."

"You let them out together when I wasn't here?" All Zoey's instincts were screaming at her that something bad was going to happen. A disaster.

Don't think. Follow the plan. Kate's voice. But Kate wasn't available. And the plan had been for Casper and Alexandra to mate.

Martha laughed a fake little trilling laugh. "They've got to get together sometime."

If Zoey were going to confront the older woman, now was the moment. "No, they don't. That dog isn't Alexandra, is it? I heard you call her Cleo. That's Alexandra's sister."

Martha blinked three times. Zoey counted. "Of—of course it's Cleopatra."

"This is Casper from Ryka Kennels. He's here to breed with Alexandra of Thebes."

"Alexandra!" Another fake laugh. "I'm afraid there's been a misunderstanding. There are many, many more, er, established breeders who'd pay quite a lot to provide the sire for a litter from Alexandra."

Zoey believed her. That's why Kate and Ryan had waived the stud fee and absorbed who knew how much in expenses just to get Casper here. They'd wanted a puppy from the litter. They'd wanted the prestige. There had been no misunderstanding. This was good old-fashioned bait and switch.

"Casper is already a champion, and he's just getting started. My sister would never have put him through this trip for a hookup with a no-name." Maybe she would have been more diplomatic if Martha hadn't been staring down her nose like Casper at his most disdainful.

"How dare you! Your sister should be grateful for the chance to have a Merriweather puppy!"

"She may be, but I can't ask her because she's on a plane right now. So until I can, I want Casper back inside." Zoey headed for the human door on the side of the building.

Before she reached it, one of the dogs yelped, a horrible sound that made Zoey's blood freeze.

"Cleo!" Martha streaked past her out the door.

Zoey ran after her, wondering if Martha was worried that Cleo had been hurt or had done the hurting.

As soon as she spotted the dogs, Zoey searched for signs of red on a white coat. The dogs were circling each other warily before flinging themselves at each other on their hind legs in a snarling dance.

"Casper!" Zoey darted toward him.

Martha grabbed her arm. "They're just playing."

Zoey shook off Martha's hand. "It sounds like they're going to bite each other's head off."

"It's part of the courtship."

"Well, I'm calling a time-out." Zoey approached the gate to the enclosure.

"Leave them alone!" Martha ordered.

As Zoey watched, the dogs chased each other before Cleo stood her ground and snapped at Casper.

Okay. That was it. "I want Casper out of there until I can talk to my sister." Zoey tugged at the gate, but it was locked. She looked at Martha.

"If you insist on separating them now, then there will be no second chance to breed with Cleo or any other Merriweather dog. Ever." Martha's grim face reminded Zoey of an evil witch casting a curse.

Zoey hesitated.

Don't think. Her sister's voice.

Sometimes people have so much invested they'll agree

to a bad deal rather than walking away empty-handed. But sometimes, you've got to walk. Cam's voice.

"Unlock the gate." As she said the words, Zoey knew she'd made the right decision.

"As you wish." Tight-lipped, Martha opened the gate and gestured Zoey inside.

Great. Now how was she supposed to catch Casper? Obviously, she couldn't depend on Martha to help her.

The two dogs were running full-tilt alongside each other. For a moment, Zoey admired their rippling coats—until they ran straight toward her.

"Casper!" Zoey jumped aside.

He didn't even slow. They ran right past Zoey, who whipped around in time to see them heading for Martha, who stood next to a wide-open gate.

"Hey!" Zoey pointed. "They're going to get out!"

But as she watched first Cleo and then Casper streak through the opening, Zoey realized that was exactly what Martha had intended.

"Don't worry, the entire property is fenced," Martha called as Zoey ran past her.

"That's no help!" she flung over her shoulder. "Casper! Come here!" she yelled, but the dogs were galloping away. Zoey jogged to a stop. No way was she going to catch them until they wanted to be caught.

Her breath puffed white clouds in front of her, but Zoey was too upset to feel the cold. After spending days cooped up, Casper would be enjoying this chance to run free, even without a female in heat. But the clumps of grass beneath Zoey's boots were hard, and the short, scrubby bushes were just waiting to claw at Casper's silky coat.

It was inconceivable that the owner of the legendary Merriweather Kennels would pull a stunt like this to take out the competition, but that's the way it looked to Zoey. It would be a miracle if Casper escaped without injury.

She already knew how the story would play out. Martha would claim it was an accident, and with the power of the Merriweather reputation behind her, people would believe her, especially because Zoey had no experience.

Martha would blame her. Zoey could already write the script. "If you'd sent someone with *any* experience at all…"

The dogs, so far away Zoey couldn't tell which was which, stopped running, faced each other for several seconds and then abruptly took off back the way they'd come.

"Casper!" Zoey patted her knees, hoping against hope that he'd come to her. "Come here, Casper!" she called frantically. "Treat! Want a treat? Chew toy! Come get a chew toy!"

Without breaking stride, he raced past.

Zoey gasped at his dirty legs and the grasses and twigs clinging to his coat.

Cleo didn't look any better, but Cleo wasn't headed for a major dog show next week, was she?

The dogs made another lap and again Zoey tried to get Casper to come to her.

Martha had walked over to the side exercise yard where she'd put the other dogs. They'd started barking and carrying on when they saw Casper and Cleo running free. She wasn't even attempting to corral Cleo.

"*Casper,* come here!" Zoey screamed so loud her throat hurt, but he ignored her.

A whistle pierced the air and both dogs stopped. It sounded again and Zoey heard a familiar voice call, "Casper!"

"Cam?" He stood outside the enclosure by the front driveway.

Casper galloped toward him and flung himself at the fence in an attempt to get to Cam.

Cam knelt and fussed over Casper, giving Zoey a chance to run and grab his collar.

"What are you doing here?"

He stood. "I tried to call but your phone was off."

"I never plugged it in. But you're supposed to be at your meeting!"

"Never mind that. Are you okay? Is Casper okay?"

"I'm fine." She looked down at the panting dog. "He seems fine, too. His coat's trashed, though. But why did you come back?"

Cam looked over her shoulder, and Zoey heard footsteps approaching. "I met Alexandra of Thebes."

Zoey sat in the back of the SUV with Casper and picked bits and pieces of Yakima Valley landscape out of his coat.

Martha had offered Zoey some of Merriweather's "Rescue Coat." When she'd refused, the older woman had handed Zoey back the gift basket and predicted that some of the debris would have to be cut out. She didn't appear all that broken up about it, either.

And speaking of broken up... Cam had torpedoed his meeting to rescue her, so not only had Zoey caused a disaster for Kate, but also Cam. Two at once. How very efficient of her.

Yeah. She was a real success at being a failure.

She heard a faint beeping sound. Oh, goody. Her phone was charged. Now she could tell Kate the news.

Cam unplugged it from the cigarette lighter and silently passed the phone, cord and all, to her.

Then he plugged his own phone in to charge. "I have video."

It was the first either of them had spoken for an hour.

Zoey had been so upset, she'd been afraid she'd say things she didn't mean. Or things she did mean but shouldn't say. Cam had related the whole story, but in the end it came down to Cam riding to the rescue because he didn't believe Zoey could handle the situation on her own. Well, she'd handled it, but maybe not the way Kate would have.

"I don't have to see the video. I believe you." That wasn't the point.

"Your sister might need to see it."

"So she won't hate me forever? Cam to the rescue again."

"Zoey." He exhaled. "This wasn't—"

"Don't you *dare* say it wasn't my fault!"

His eyes met hers in the rearview mirror before flicking toward the road. "This wasn't a rescue and it wasn't completely about you. Not only were they committing fraud, Casper could have been hurt. Even knowing that, I kept driving, reminding myself that you'd be there watching and were smart enough to sense when something was wrong. But *you* could have been hurt protecting Casper. And Zoey, if that had happened, I wouldn't have been able to live with myself. There was no way I'd be in the best frame of mind for meeting with a shark like Richard. So I made the choice to turn around. I knew how it would seem to you, and I knew you'd be mad, but I *chose* to come back to give you information you needed. And I'd expect you to do the same for me."

"As though *you'll* ever need rescuing."

"Not a rescue," he insisted. "It's called working together, being there for each other, lightening the load, supporting—"

"Okay, I get it."

"I hope so." Cam pulled the car onto a dirt road marked by a colorful wooden sign advertising the hops farm. "Because I hate all these rules and secret tests you have to determine how you value yourself. It's like walking through a minefield and being afraid that at any second something will blow up in my face. I don't want the responsibility for your self-esteem. I believe in you, but that doesn't matter if you don't believe in yourself."

"Cam!" Zoey felt as though she'd been slapped in the face with a wet washcloth.

"What?"

Yeah, what? "I—I don't know what to say."

"You didn't think I could get mad? I get mad."

In the mirror, she saw him scowl. "It doesn't mean I don't love you."

Just when she thought she couldn't feel worse, he said those horrible, awful things to her. And the reason they were horrible and awful was because they were true.

Zoey stared out the window at miles of bare metal arches waiting to support the next season of hops. "I'm a mess."

"Yeah, but you're my mess."

He said it with such a gruff tenderness that Zoey burst into tears. "I don't deserve you," she wailed. "And you don't deserve to get stuck with me!"

"Zoey," he said in a strange voice. "Would you mind if I convince you you're being totally ridiculous later?"

"What?" She sniffed.

They were approaching a metal building. Cam gestured to a blue sedan bearing a local airport's logo. "Richard is still here."

AFTER TEN MINUTES, Cam wished Richard *hadn't* still been there. Clearly, he'd stayed only to embarrass and berate Cam any way he could. He hadn't changed much from the unpleasantly arrogant student Cam remembered. He'd had his teeth fixed, wore expensive clothes and probably worked out with a trainer, but until he had a personality transplant, all the money in the world wouldn't make people enjoy his company.

The way things were going, Cam wouldn't have been surprised if Richard had dumped Cam's samples in the trash in front of him, so instead, Cam had presented the box to Don, the farm's manager, who appeared genuinely pleased.

Don had taken the box and moved away, discreetly giving them the illusion of privacy, but Cam knew Richard's voice carried in the cavernous area.

Richard knew it, too. He continued to speak in a voice loud enough to echo as he methodically criticized every aspect of MacNeil's Brewery.

At least they were outside now, moving toward Richard's car. Cam checked the SUV and saw that it was empty. Zoey must be walking Casper.

Richard was making a show of putting on driving gloves. They were probably expensive. Cam didn't know and didn't care.

"At first, I was willing to drop a generous amount of cash into your brewery in return for my own private-label beer. After you missed our initial meeting, I wasn't feeling quite so generous, although it did give me the opportunity to do a little research."

"Yes. My cousin told me."

"Your cousin was rude to my team."

"Your team didn't inform anyone they were coming."

"I find surprise visits yield more information," Richard said with irritating condescension. Did he *want* people to hate him?

"And this morning I found myself with time to act on that information." Richard finished putting on his gloves and gave Cam a small, smug smile. "I do hate to waste time, and since you didn't appear interested in meeting with me, I bought the Beer Barn."

"You're the one who bid on their tanks?" Cam should have known.

"Yes. And then I thought, just buy the whole place. So I did."

Richard was watching for Cam's reaction, but he was determined not to show his disappointment. "Congratulations. It's a popular spot." *But it won't stay that way with you in charge.*

"You were in negotiations to brew the house beer, I understand."

"Which you'll want to be your private label." Now it wouldn't be a MacNeil's brew, which was a disappointment, but Cam could live with that.

"Absolutely. I want there to be a guaranteed supply, and your brewery is on shaky ground. However, I'm still willing to allow you to supply the beer on the condition that I install my own management team." He handed Cam a piece of paper outlining his terms and the amount he was willing to invest.

The money was more than Cam had dreamed, but that team would make Cam's life miserable. Which was, of course, exactly what Richard had intended.

Cam regretted ever approaching him. "Thank you, and we'll consider your offer—"

"The offer is only valid until I get into the car." Richard was clearly enjoying this. "And, Cam, if you want to remain in business, you should take it."

Richard blipped the lock on the car and started to walk toward it when something caught his attention. He stared, his eyes unblinking.

Cam turned, and there was Zoey with Casper. The dog

was surprisingly show-worthy, considering the condition of his fur when he'd left Merriweather. But Zoey...Zoey was a vision. She'd left off her coat and must be cold, but she sure looked hot. She wore a sweater that hugged her curves, curves Cam was intimately familiar with. The sun haloed the same glossy hair that had curtained them when they'd made love. Her jeans fit snugly over her thighs and were tucked into her boots. Both he and Richard watched her hips sway hypnotically as she walked toward them, but Cam was the only one who wondered if she was wearing turquoise underwear. He didn't want to know what Richard was thinking. When she got closer, she flashed Cam a blindingly brilliant smile that dazzled him momentarily, and then she directed it at Richard, who probably short-circuited.

She glanced inquiringly at Cam. "Is this Richard? The one you said was smarter than all your friends put together?" She passed Cam Casper's leash.

"Cam said that?" Richard blinked, clearly pleased.

No, Cam had not said that.

"I'm Zoey." She stuck out her hand. "Skin Garden Organic Skin Care?" Richard nodded as though he'd heard of it.

They shook hands, but then Zoey grasped his in both of hers and drew it dangerously close to her chest—a fact Richard couldn't help but notice. Cam certainly did.

"It's my fault we're late. We were doing a product demo at Merriweather Kennels—you've heard of them? They raise champion Afghan hounds, such as Casper here."

They all looked down at Casper, who sat regally, as though a couple of hours ago he hadn't been running about like a wild thing. In fact, one side of him was still covered in grass and twigs.

"It's obvious on which side we used Skin Garden Hair Silk," Zoey said.

Cam happened to know she'd in fact soaked all of Casper in it.

"I see," Richard said.

"Anyway, it took longer than I thought and I am so, so, *so* sorry we made you wait." With each "so" she bounced Richard's hand.

"Cam probably blamed himself, but you mustn't listen to him because it was totally my fault." She tilted her head to one side and gazed at Richard imploringly. "Can you forgive me?"

"Of—of course." Richard patted her clasped hands, bringing the entire hand bundle into the red zone.

"Oh, thank you!" Distracting him with another dazzling smile, she extracted herself from Richard's grasp.

Very smoothly done.

For the next several minutes, she flattered and flirted with Richard as she chatted about expanding her product line to include the use of hops and spent grain.

Noon came and went.

She asked Richard's advice and hung on his answers as though he imparted the secrets of the universe. She was being so obvious; Richard surely could see he was being played.

But apparently not.

"Excuse me, Mr. Campbell." A man in a uniform approached Richard. "To maintain your schedule in Seattle, we must depart immediately."

Richard blinked as though coming out of a trance. Cam understood how he felt.

"Oh, do you have to go?" she asked, looking adorably devastated.

Richard nodded, looking a little devastated, himself. "I wish I could stay and give you more advice."

"You've already given me so much to consider," Zoey said with a straight face.

Richard turned to Cam. "I need your answer."

Had he noticed that Cam had not said one word since Zoey appeared? "Richard has agreed to invest, but only if he can run the place," he told her.

"That's not—" Richard began.

"Oh, no!" Zoey looked shocked and upset. Maybe she actually was. Cam was pretty shocked and upset, come to think of it.

She glanced at Richard, and then back at Cam and shook her head. "That's not going to work for me."

"I wasn't aware—" Richard began.

"Richard," she interrupted. "Cameron and I have reached a preliminary agreement—you remember how we were just talking about a skin-care line using beer by-products?"

"Yes."

"I want to source exclusively from MacNeil's Highland Beer brewery, but not if it's going to be run by someone who isn't on site." She gazed regretfully at Cam. "I've worked with companies like that and it's a nightmare having to get approval for every little thing. I won't do it again."

Cam had no idea where Zoey was coming up with this stuff, but she'd given him a way out that also prevented Richard from getting vindictive. Of course, turning him down meant no money for office help and no time for her. Did she realize that? Did she care?

"Poor Cam." Richard's eyes glittered with malicious amusement. "Money or beauty. What a choice." He turned to Zoey. "Sorry to play the money card. I do wish you luck, and if you change your mind, call me and we'll see what we can work out." His eyes roamed over her in a way that roused those caveman instincts Cam had so recently discovered he had. "I'm always seeking investment opportunities."

Casper growled. What a smart dog.

"Thank you, Richard," Zoey said with a slight bow of her head.

He lapped it up. "Cam, do we have an agreement?"

Before Cam could answer, Zoey stepped in front of him. Winding her arms around Cam's neck, she said, "Cam, before you choose, I want you to know that I love you and that's not going to change."

His heart thudded and all he could hear was the blood pulsing in his ears. She wasn't kidding, was she? Not about that.

She read the doubt in his eyes and made an exasperated face Richard couldn't see before giving Cam a slight confirming nod.

His mouth stretched into a huge smile he was helpless to control.

"I want you to choose what's best for your business." And then she tugged his head down to hers and kissed him—a full on, no-holding-back, wet whopper of a kiss that made him forget where he was.

She pulled away. "Whatever you decide, I'll understand." She accompanied this with a tremulous little smile, glanced at Richard so he'd be sure to notice it and took Casper's leash from Cam's unresisting hand.

That little quiver on her lips killed it. Killed. It.

Of course, now she'd never be able to use it on him. Fortunately.

"Come on, Casper," she said. "We're going to walk."

Going to walk. That was a message to him, not that he needed it.

Facing Richard, he drew a deep breath, but Richard held up his hand.

"We both know when a woman says you have a choice, you really don't." He stared after Zoey. "Damn. She played the love card. Did not see that coming." But he smiled as he said it. "Good luck with that one, Cam. No hard feelings, I hope. It was just business." He shook Cam's hand before jogging to the waiting car and speeding away.

Cam stood staring after him and tried to process everything that had just happened.

Zoey and Casper came running up. She'd put on her coat. "What happened?"

"You. You happened." Cam hugged her to him.

"I was awesome, wasn't I?"

"You were scary awesome. Did you just make that stuff up on the fly?"

"Yes!" She was so excited she was bouncing on her toes. "I heard what he said to you, and then he made those threats and I knew he had you backed into a corner. I just got so mad that I—"

"Came to my rescue?"

"Yep. And you played along."

He'd stayed out of her way. "It was very instructive. And, again, scary to watch you manipulate him."

"He's obviously desperate for people to recognize and admire his innate superiority. So that's what I did."

"It didn't hurt that you looked really hot while doing it."

She grinned and looped her arms around his neck the way she had a few minutes ago. "The part about loving you? I meant that."

"I know." Cam touched his forehead to hers. "So did

Richard. That's what really sold it. That and the little—"
He indicated her mouth. "Lip thing."

She made her lip quiver before laughing. "Did you turn him down?"

"I didn't have to. He assumed I would and left. Thanks to you, he seemed okay with it, so I don't think he'll bother running us out of business. Of course, that also means no cash unless Gus pulls off a miracle with the family. But, Zoey, the important thing is that you turned my mistake into a success. You realize that, don't you?"

She nodded. "I'm two-for-two today. I talked with Kate and they'd both heard of the incident with Cleo. When I told Kate what happened today, she started sobbing and at first I thought she was mad, but she thanked me about a gazillion times. She also said she was glad I'd stood up to Martha because she probably would have caved to avoid offending her. So, yay me."

She seemed so pleased with herself Cam couldn't help kissing her.

After kissing him back for a few seconds, Zoey said, "You realize that you have to insist on getting more help at the brewery, right? You're entitled to a life outside work. And in the interests of full disclosure, I'm hoping you'll spend part of that life with me."

He smiled. "I do realize. Even though Richard was being a jerk, most of what he said was true."

"Joyce said a lot of the same things," Zoey pointed out.

"Okay, okay. I'll hire someone. The financing will be tricky, but we'll make it work."

"I'll help." Zoey stood on her toes to kiss him and swayed. "I think the adrenaline is wearing off. I'm about to fall asleep standing up."

"Ordinarily, I'd be offended if a woman fell asleep while I was kissing her, but a bed sounds really good right now."

Casper barked as if in agreement, which made them laugh. Arms linked, they were about to head to the car when Don, the farm manager, called to them. "So are you folks ready for the tour?"

Cam had completely forgotten. "Ah…"

"Sure," Zoey answered Don. "I'm especially interested in the cosmetic properties of hops." Looking up at Cam she whispered, "We've got the rest of our lives to sleep."

Fifteen Months Later

"YER BOTH DAFT. First you have a dog stand up for you at your wedding, and then you postpone your honeymoon to go watch him prance around a ring." Gus shook his head. "It's not normal."

Zoey grinned at her husband over Gus's bowed head.

"I wouldn't have met Zoey if it hadn't been for Casper," Cam reminded him. "And if I recall, he behaved better at the wedding than you did."

"Aye, that's a fact," Gus admitted.

"This could be his big moment, Gus," Zoey said. "He's only three points away from becoming a Grand Champion, and he should pick them up this weekend."

It would be exciting, but no win would ever be as sweet as the one where he'd been named breed champion over Alexandra of Thebes the week after his awful visit to Merriweather.

Martha Merriweather had agreed to "retire" rather than have what she'd done made public, and Sheryl and her husband were now in charge of the kennel and breeding program. Alexandra had also retired and had a litter of puppies, one of which was owned by Ryka Kennels, and was growing up alongside Zoey's baby niece.

Joyce came up to them, an envelope in her hands. "I

have the volunteer schedule set up and have Shanna filling the online orders for the Highland Beer Garden products. Cam's brothers will be taking on brewer's duties while you're on your honeymoon, and I will handle payroll." Joyce handed Zoey the envelope. "I printed out your tickets and a limousine will drive you to the airport, compliments of MacNeil's Highland Beer."

"Thank you, Joyce," Zoey said and impulsively hugged her. "I don't know what we'd do without you."

"I do, and it still gives me nightmares." Joyce gave a mock shudder.

Zoey laughed. After Gus had convinced the family to invest enough money to hire an office manager, it had been Zoey's idea to hire Joyce, and it had been the best idea she'd ever had. Joyce had been so excited when they'd asked her to be the office manager, she'd moved to Texas from Florida within a week. On Thursday nights at the brewery, she taught a free course for small-business owners. The rest of the time, she kept them all organized. Profits had increased enough to hire more employees. Gus professed to be frightened of her, which Zoey didn't think was a bad thing.

Best of all—well, second best of all—was that Zoey had quit her job in the customer-service call center to concentrate on her skin-care products.

And the very best was that Zoey's string of failures had not only ended when she met Cam, her current string of successes had begun.

She walked over to him and slipped her arm around his waist.

He smiled, flashing those dimples she loved. "Ready?"

She nodded. "For anything."

* * * * *

COMING NEXT MONTH FROM

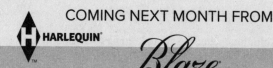

HARLEQUIN
Blaze

Available July 15, 2014

#807 RIDING HOME
Sons of Chance
by Vicki Lewis Thompson

Zach Powell has left the law for ranch life. He's just the cowboy to help perfectionist lawyer Jeannette Trenton learn to forgive herself—and let loose. But one wild weekend isn't enough to satisfy their desire....

#808 DARE ME
It's Trading Men!
by Jo Leigh

Wine expert Molly Webster craves the finer things in life, but one taste of master brewer Cameron Crawford sends her into sensory overload. Too bad their chemistry can only last one night!

#809 COMMAND CONTROL
Uniformly Hot!
by Sara Jane Stone

Erotica writer Sadie Bannerman is just looking for one good man...who doesn't mind being tied up. And dangerously hot Army Ranger Logan Reed is reporting for duty!

#810 THE MIGHTY QUINNS: ROGAN
The Mighty Quinns
by Kate Hoffmann

Straight-laced psychologist Claudia Mathison is determined to unearth sexy adventure guide Rogan Quinn's deepest secrets. But Rogan figures the best way to keep her out of his head is to keep her *in* his bed.

YOU CAN FIND MORE INFORMATION ON UPCOMING HARLEQUIN® TITLES, FREE EXCERPTS AND MORE AT WWW.HARLEQUIN.COM.

HBCNM0714

REQUEST YOUR FREE BOOKS!
2 FREE NOVELS PLUS 2 FREE GIFTS!

HARLEQUIN Blaze®

red-hot reads!

YES! Please send me 2 FREE Harlequin® Blaze™ novels and my 2 FREE gifts (gifts are worth about $10). After receiving them, if I don't wish to receive any more books, I can return the shipping statement marked "cancel." If I don't cancel, I will receive 4 brand-new novels every month and be billed just $4.74 per book in the U.S. or $4.96 per book in Canada. That's a savings of at least 14% off the cover price. It's quite a bargain. Shipping and handling is just 50¢ per book in the U.S. and 75¢ per book in Canada.* I understand that accepting the 2 free books and gifts places me under no obligation to buy anything. I can always return a shipment and cancel at any time. Even if I never buy another book, the two free books and gifts are mine to keep forever.

150/350 HDN F4WC

Name _____ (PLEASE PRINT) _____

Address _____ Apt. # _____

City _____ State/Prov. _____ Zip/Postal Code _____

Signature (if under 18, a parent or guardian must sign) _____

Mail to the **Harlequin® Reader Service:**
IN U.S.A.: P.O. Box 1867, Buffalo, NY 14240-1867
IN CANADA: P.O. Box 609, Fort Erie, Ontario L2A 5X3

Want to try two free books from another line?
Call 1-800-873-8635 or visit www.ReaderService.com.

* Terms and prices subject to change without notice. Prices do not include applicable taxes. Sales tax applicable in N.Y. Canadian residents will be charged applicable taxes. Offer not valid in Quebec. This offer is limited to one order per household. Not valid for current subscribers to Harlequin Blaze books. All orders subject to credit approval. Credit or debit balances in a customer's account(s) may be offset by any other outstanding balance owed by or to the customer. Please allow 4 to 6 weeks for delivery. Offer available while quantities last.

Your Privacy—The Harlequin® Reader Service is committed to protecting your privacy. Our Privacy Policy is available online at www.ReaderService.com or upon request from the Harlequin Reader Service.

We make a portion of our mailing list available to reputable third parties that offer products we believe may interest you. If you prefer that we not exchange your name with third parties, or if you wish to clarify or modify your communication preferences, please visit us at www.ReaderService.com/consumerchoice or write to us at Harlequin Reader Service Preference Service, P.O. Box 9062, Buffalo, NY 14269. Include your complete name and address.

HB13R2

SPECIAL EXCERPT FROM

Enjoy a sizzling sneak peek of

Command Control

by Sara Jane Stone—the latest in the
reader-favorite *Uniformly Hot!* miniseries!

After more than a decade in the army, Logan knew when to
withdraw and wait for the enemy to pass. Opening the door
to Main Street Books, he slipped inside. He found a position
deep in the maze of bookshelves. Pulling the nearest book from
the shelf, he pretended to read the back cover.

"If you need assistance picking out a romance novel, I can
help."

His gaze snapped to the redhead standing two feet away.
The desire he'd felt when he'd seen her the day before returned
full force.

"But if it's your first time—" she continued "—you might
want to steer clear of erotica."

"Erotica?" Logan glanced at the book in his hand. On the
front cover was a practically nude woman lying on a bed.
A man in leather pants stood next to her holding a whip.
Not what he'd expect to find on the shelf in his hometown.
"Mount Pleasant sells erotica?"

"Not much," she said grimly. "But what they do have is
pretty good."

She stepped toward him and reached for a book on the shelf
above his head. The side of her breast brushed his arm, sending
a red-alert signal through his body.

"If you're looking for a classic romance, this is one of my
favorites." She held out a copy of a Jane Austen novel.

HBEXP79813

He shook his head. "Read that one in high school. It wasn't for me."

She placed the book on the shelf and turned to him, her eyes sparkling with amusement. "To find the perfect romance, I'll need to know a little bit more about you."

"Not much to tell. I'm home on leave."

"You're a soldier?" Her smile widened. "Let me guess. Special Forces."

"Army ranger."

"No kidding?" Laughing, she scanned the shelves before selecting another paperback. "This one should be just right for you."

She handed him the book. The cover showed a man with a naked chest, dog tags hanging around his neck.

"He's a SEAL, and she's a nurse," she said. "They have hot sex, overcome a few challenges and fall in love."

"The hot sex part sounds good." He set the book back on the shelf. "But I'm not looking for a fairy-tale ending."

She handed him back the first book. "Then maybe you should stick with erotica."

Her fingers touched his and lingered. He glanced up at her and saw the heat in her eyes. Whatever was happening here wasn't one-sided. He shook his head. "I'm not into whips."

"What if I told you I could convince you to give it a try?"

"Are you really into—"

"No, I was teasing. Whips aren't my thing," she said, smiling. "And I'm Sadie."

"Logan." He ran a hand over the back of his neck. "But now I'm curious how you'd convince me…."

Pick up COMMAND CONTROL by Sara Jane Stone, on sale August 2014 wherever Harlequin® Blaze® books and ebooks are sold.

HBEXP79813

Saddle up for a wild ride!

Zach Powell has left the law for ranch life. He's just the cowboy to help perfectionist lawyer Jeannette Trenton learn to forgive herself—and let loose. But one wild weekend isn't enough to satisfy their desire....

Don't miss the final chapter of the **Sons of Chance** trilogy

Riding Home

from *New York Times* bestselling author

Vicki Lewis Thompson

Available August 2014 wherever you buy Harlequin Blaze books.

Red-Hot Reads
www.Harlequin.com

HB79811